"There's still the question of whether we can work together," Jake said.

Maria started to say something, but the words caught in her throat. He watched, mesmerized, as her tongue flicked out to moisten her lips. She swallowed hard, then nodded.

Jake was shaken to the core of his being. Maria Santos, of the cool, competent manner, translucent skin, and lithe grace, had given the slightest, most reluctant signal that she wanted him. The realization swept through him with the force of a tidal wave. He'd never wanted a woman this much, as sailors three thousand years ago had wanted the sirens who sang to them from the rocks.

"I think it's worth a try," he murmured. Then he pulled her against him, and brought his lips to meet hers. . . .

WHAT ARE *LOVESWEPT* ROMANCES?

They are stories of true romance and touching emotion. We believe those two very important ingredients are constants in our highly sensual and very believable stories in the *LOVESWEPT* line. Our goal is to give you, the reader, stories of consistently high quality that may sometimes make you laugh, sometimes make you cry, but are always fresh and creative and contain many delightful surprises within their pages.

Most romance fans read an enormous number of books. Those they truly love, they keep. Others may be traded with friends and soon forgotten. We hope that each *LOVESWEPT* romance will be a treasure—a "keeper." We will always try to publish

LOVE STORIES YOU'LL NEVER FORGET
BY AUTHORS YOU'LL ALWAYS REMEMBER

The Editors

Loveswept ® 616

Linda Warren
Swept Away

BANTAM BOOKS

NEW YORK · TORONTO · LONDON · SYDNEY · AUCKLAND

SWEPT AWAY

A Bantam Book / May 1993

If you would be interested in receiving protective vinyl
covers for your Loveswept books, please write to this
address for information:

Loveswept
Bantam Books
P.O. Box 985
Hicksville, NY 11802

ISBN 0-553-44209-0

Published simultaneously in the United States and Canada

PRINTED IN THE UNITED STATES OF AMERICA

OPM   0 9 8 7 6 5 4 3 2 1

One

Maria Santos cut the diesels and slowed to four knots as she came into Gull Cove harbor. All the way in she had fought an offshore breeze, a slight chop, and a stiff resentment against the obligation that called her home. Behind her was Stellwagon Bank, the North Atlantic's richest feeding grounds for fish, seabirds, and humpback whales. In front of her, standing and waiting on the Marlow Whale Watching dock, was the obligation.

She'd never met Jake Marlow, but she recognized him on first sight. He had his grandfather's broad shoulders, the blond hair and flint-blue gaze of a Yankee pirate, and enough Marlow arrogance to float a whale-watching boat. He was speaking into a cellular phone while he watched her, but as the *Spiritos* glided into her slip, he punched a button, stuffed the phone into his pocket, and propped his hands on his hips. His impeccably cut suit jacket, snagged behind his wrists, gaped over tailored trousers and an immaculate white shirt. He didn't look at his watch, but Maria could imagine his thoughts. He was here to assess her competence, and she was five and a third minutes late.

"Ms. Santos?" The voice was cool, deep, and skeptical, a perfect match for his arrogant gaze, and Maria found herself quelling a small, electric shiver that wanted to chase down her spine.

Being manager of Wyatt Marlow's whale-watching fleet had its rewards, but she had a premonition that passing muster with his grandson wasn't one of them. She met Jake Marlow's hard blue eyes through the open window of the wheelhouse, then forced herself to square her shoulders and step out on deck. "Yes," she said, "I'm Maria Santos." She reached for the bowline and straightened with the rope in her hands. "I apologize for being late, Mr. Marlow. There were nineteen humpbacks off Stellwagon. I couldn't start the engines without the risk of running them down."

He frowned at her across six feet of harbor water. "You couldn't get back here because you were surrounded by whales?"

She didn't have an immediate answer to the cynical, dubious question. Perhaps because the answer was a simple yes, and she had the unnerving impression that Jake Marlow wasn't prepared to accept it. Everything about the man, in fact, was unnerving. When she'd spoken to him over the phone, she'd been calm, objective, sure of herself. But the phone didn't convey the whole impact of Jake Marlow's physical presence.

She hefted the wet bowline and glanced along the dock for one of the mates to help her secure the boat. No mate in sight. She muttered a Portuguese irreverence.

"My thoughts exactly," Jake said through his teeth.

She felt a rush of color in her face. The man had the hearing of a sonar scanner! "The whales were within twenty yards of my boat, Mr. Marlow," she explained. "The Marine Mammals Protection Act clearly—"

He cut her off with a cursory wave of one hand, and his mouth quirked in an odd smile that was almost—before he spoke again—appealing. "Clearly the marine mammals weren't the ones who needed protection."

Maria tightened her grip on the rope and her hold on her fraying temper. She wasn't normally given to anger, but nothing about this situation was normal. She was late, she was wearing a faded jersey and jeans for an appointment she'd planned to keep in professional dress, and unless one of the mates materialized soon, she'd end up scrambling around like a first-season deckhand trying to dock her boat!

As if he'd read her mind, his gaze swept down the *Spiritos*'s forty-foot length, then moved back to her. "Did you go out by yourself?" he asked with a touch of disbelief.

"Yes. The *Spiritos* is my boat. I've been taking her out by myself for years."

His eyes flicked down over her slight figure. Her French-braided hair was caught over one shoulder, and as she leaned away from the counterweight of the heavy bowline, her jersey pulled taut across her breasts.

Maria felt an unfamiliar surge of defensiveness color her cheekbones. What he thought of her physical attributes didn't make the least bit of difference, she told herself. But his implied opinion of her seamanship unsettled her. She'd been hired two months earlier, after Wyatt's heart attack had forced him into retirement, because she was experienced at running her own boat and her own business. She didn't like giving the impression of incompetence. "You don't have to worry about the Marlow boats," she assured him brusquely. "They don't go out without a full crew."

"I'm glad to hear it." He looked down the length of the dock beyond the *Spiritos*, empty except for the Marlow's harbor dinghy and Maria's dory. Maria followed his gaze, shifting the line in her hands, wishing she'd assigned one of the mates to stand by when she came in, even if that meant a whole afternoon's work neglected.

There was no one on the dock but Jake Marlow. His silk tie fluttered in the same breeze that threatened to blow the *Spiritos* back out into the harbor. His Italian loafers were planted firmly on the salt-rimed boards.

"Stand by, Mr. Marlow," she called out on impulse. "Catch!" She knew how to heave a line. She aimed it straight for his gold tie tack.

His head snapped around at the last moment, just before the coiled line hit him in the rib cage. He staggered back two steps, off balance. For a horrified, repentant moment Maria thought he was going to topple backward into the harbor, but he caught himself on one heel, and his hands closed automatically around the line.

The look he shot her could have bored through the hull of one of the Marlow boats. A mass of damp lash lines darkened his shirt and plastered it to his skin, and across the fly of his pleated trousers a dark, wet line angled toward his thigh. His jaw was clenched as though the words that might come out of his mouth were too dangerous to let loose, and even beneath the skillfully tailored jacket she could see the muscles of his shoulders bunch in tense reaction.

Maria felt a sharp bolt of regret at her own misguided impulse. Jake Marlow not only owned thirty percent of the Marlow fleet, he owned the Marine insurance agency that underwrote it. And she'd nearly knocked him into the next liability claim she had to file!

She searched for belated words of apology, but he merely shifted his angry gaze to the rope in his hands and rearranged the coils with a single, adroit heave. He crossed the dock to the piling, where, to her surprise, he made the line fast with two efficient turns.

Chastened, she moved down the side deck, threw out the stern line, then scrambled over the side of the boat after it. She landed with lithe, easy grace on the floating catwalk.

Jake had the second line secured before she could reach it. When he straightened from the task, he wiped his hands deliberately on his trousers and crossed his arms in front of his chest.

She waited for his rebuke, taking in his strong, angular face, the nose that had been broken at least once, the stubborn, square jaw that suited both his face and his nature. There was no point in apologizing, she realized, looking into those cynical blue eyes. He wouldn't believe she was sorry.

But his mouth quirked again in the singular Marlow way that conveyed something amusing and unbelievable at the same time, and she got a sudden, surprised glimpse of a sense of humor she wouldn't have expected.

The change unsettled her almost as much as his original abruptness. It transformed his gaze from cynical, business-sharp perception to something warmer, more magnetic, far more appealing.

Almost too appealing to look away from. She realized, surprised at herself, that she was staring. And from the subtle change in his expression, she knew he realized it as well. A sensual awareness, like a high-frequency hum just within audible range, vibrated along her nerve endings, surprising her and raising a warning she didn't often need. This wasn't a situation that allowed for sensual entanglements.

She pulled her gaze away from his, stopped herself by force of will from stepping back from him, and pushed her hands into the pockets of her jeans. "You wanted this meeting, Mr. Marlow," she said with more control than she felt. "You chose the place and the time. I'm here."

"That makes two of us." A single careless glance assessed his wet shirt and pants. "I don't recall specifying that we stand out in the wind, though. Maybe we could walk down to the office and get a cup of coffee."

"All right." She turned shoreward toward the faded metal building that served as the Whale Watching office and ticket-sales window.

Jake followed Maria, his gaze on her slim, graceful back, his mind on the way she'd hit him with a hundred feet of rope. It was a pretty accurate metaphor for her effect on him: unexpected, immediate, a hair's breadth from knocking him into the drink. The lithe, feminine body beneath the fisherman's clothes hinted at ideas that could stir a man's imagination. Raven-dark hair, translucent skin, eyes that suggested equal amounts of innocence and ancient wisdom. And something more, something he'd forgotten, or suppressed, in the last ten years of his life. Her quick grace, her direct, truthful manner, the softness of consonants indicated, to someone attuned to it, a Portuguese background. She took him back to the sea.

Her hair, braided down the back of her head, hung in a thick coil between her shoulder blades, barely swinging with each long, graceful sailor's stride. Without breaking the rhythm of her walk she stepped up from the catwalk to the dock, one slim hand resting on the piling. She gave him a brief glance over her shoulder. "Would you prefer to go up to the house? Mrs. Salintes, the housekeeper, always has coffee on."

"No," he said.

Her brief look was just barely quizzical. She didn't have to ask why he didn't want to go to the house, Jake thought. She knew his grandfather. Without comment she started down the dock, past the empty slips where the hundred-foot Marlow boats would be tied up at the end of their working day.

The harbor water lapped rhythmically at his memory. The dock smelled of salt and seaweed. He could feel the rough, wet weight of line she'd hit him with, and the sensation brought back with startling, disturbing clarity his days of working the fleet. With one unexpected act Maria Santos had thrust those coils of memory into his hands and pulled him back to something he'd never intended to return to.

He didn't intend it now, he reminded himself, despite the fire Maria Santos stirred in his body. The attraction he felt for her was the kind that called inexperienced sailors into treacherous waters, but he wasn't an inexperienced sailor, and he had no intention of facing shipwreck. He was there to do a job. To see to the welfare of a two-million-dollar investment that had paid back in satisfyingly measurable percentages while Wyatt had been running the fleet. Jake planned to see they stayed that way.

His grandfather's new manager shot him another

look and, with no preamble, gave voice to his own train of thought. "Is this about the last liability claim I filed this spring, Mr. Marlow?"

"Yes," he said. "As a matter of fact it is."

There was a short pause.

"I believe everything was in order on the claim."

"It was." He waited a moment, considering his words, wondering how quick Maria would be to take in the situation. "Everything was in order on the previous three claims too. Making four in the two months you've been managing the fleet."

"You don't have to remind me of it. I filed them myself."

"You should have known, then, that the agency would question them."

Sudden understanding brought a flare of color beneath her skin, dusky rose against the pale, golden clarity of her complexion. "I answered all your questions over the phone, Mr. Marlow. You didn't indicate that this would require an official investigation."

Official investigations on insurance claims weren't usually advertised to the industry being investigated, he thought sardonically, but he kept his tone of voice bland and his answer, as far as it went, true. "This isn't an official investigation."

Her finely arched brows drew together. "Then— what can I do for you, Mr. Marlow?"

"I want information, Ms. Santos."

"Information?"

"Regarding the fleet—and all its employees."

He could feel her reaction in the short, significant silence. "Mr. Marlow," she said. "I'm aware that the four liability claims—gangplank slipping, engine problems, electronics malfunction—could have been caused by sloppy maintenance, or cost-cutting measures to meet the profit margin. They weren't. I can provide you with records of fleet maintenance—"

"Fine," he said evenly. "I want the other records too. Accounts receivable, expenditures, employment records, references."

She stopped walking and turned toward him. Her dark eyes met his gaze levelly. "You'll need to talk to your grandfather, Mr. Marlow. I can't help you."

"My grandfather, Ms. Santos, is under doctor's orders to stay out of the business for at least three months."

Her shoulders squared, directly and with purpose. "Then you'll have to wait."

"It's not a matter I can wait on."

Her chin rose a notch in the direct, seafaring manner that spoke more than words. She wasn't easily placated with half a piece of information, Jake realized. He took in a breath. "Even if I could wait, talking to my grandfather isn't an option, Ms. Santos. It's no secret we don't have a working relationship. I think you probably know that."

"Yes."

"I realize you probably don't deal with my grandfather's back files. I'm not asking you to sort out the information, just to pass it on."

"I know what you're asking." She started toward the office again.

"Good. I'll see that you're compensated for any extra work you—"

"It's not a question of compensation, Mr. Marlow," she said sharply. Her sneakers slapped against the boards of the dock with angry emphasis. "It's a question of loyalty."

Jake frowned at her. She shot back the look and stepped up onto the concrete landing of the office. "I can't do it," she said, pushing at the door.

Jake's palm flattened against the door above her head as he pushed it open for her with more force than necessary.

She shot him a glance over her shoulder, chin lifted, eyes unreadable, and stepped ahead of him into the office.

"What in the name o' hell is goin' on *here*?" Wyatt Marlow snapped from behind the office desk.

For a moment no one moved. Two identical flint-blue gazes locked together with the singing pull of a taut line. Maria glanced from one to the other, then, slowly, let go of the door she'd caught on the backswing.

It banged shut.

"Well?" the elder Marlow demanded.

"How are you, Wyatt?" Jake asked, his voice ironic.

The fierce jut of his chin shot a defiant challenge across the room. "I'll be better when I get an answer."

"I doubt it, but I'll give you one anyway," his grandson said. "We're discussing an insurance claim."

Wyatt's sharp gaze flicked to Maria. "Is that true?" he demanded.

Wyatt's color was angry and florid, his fist clenched on the desk in tension his doctor would surely not approve. "Yes," she said calmly.

"You asked him to come here?"

"No."

"Then what are you doin' here?" he barked at Jake. "Your phone out of order?"

Jake's jaw clenched. "I thought it might help this particular matter if I came in person."

Wyatt snorted, and the cords of his neck stood out. "We don't need help from a man who walked out of this business ten years ago! We didn't need you here then, and we don't need you here now!"

"Bull," Jake muttered succinctly. "You wouldn't admit you needed a life preserver if you were ten miles out in a twenty-foot sea."

She could feel Wyatt's blood pressure rising like the tide, matching the angry force of his voice. "I've been ten miles out in a twenty-foot sea!" The chair rolled backward as he leaped to his feet. "I'll be there again, by God!"

Maria drew in a breath, flung her logbook down on the desk, and deliberately stepped between Wyatt and his grandson. "You won't be going anywhere in the future, Wyatt," she said evenly, "if you don't take care of yourself now."

"I am taking care of myself!"

She didn't contradict him. Wyatt, she knew from experience, would usually defer to good judgment as long as it wasn't presented as a challenge—a lesson that apparently hadn't been absorbed by his grandson.

She nodded at her employer, raising dark eyebrows. "What are you doing in the office? Your doctor said three months, Wyatt."

His square jaw clenched, and she folded her arms in front of her, feeling the crosscurrents of tension all the way down her spine.

"For two months I've been sitting up in that godda—"

Wyatt broke off the profanity, scowled at her, and took a step back toward the chair.

Maria let out a slow breath. She kept her eyes on Wyatt, but every other sense was attuned to that other blue gaze. Beneath her forced self-possession was a sharp instinct that told her she was being appraised, evaluated, and filed for future reference. She made herself ignore it.

Wyatt settled into the seat, gesturing with one arm in vigorous disgust. "I take it you've already met my grandson," he muttered.

"Yes," she said, looking at Jake. *And she wished she'd stayed out on the Bank with her whales.* Nineteen humpbacks, even if they were ten miles out in a twenty-foot sea, were preferable to being caught between Wyatt's ill health and his grandson's perplexing and unfulfillable demands. "And I appreciate why he wanted to come in person," she added diplomatically.

Wyatt snorted. "And how do you think that's supposed to help the fleet?" he inquired with sarcasm but no further ranting.

"It might simplify some of the paperwork, for one thing," Jake said levelly.

"And who wants it simplified?"

"Maria might." Jake nodded toward her, and she returned the glance without returning the nod. She hadn't missed the use of her first name. She didn't particularly like it.

Jake slid his hands casually into his pockets. The action made his jacket gape open over his wet shirt.

Wyatt's eyes narrowed as he took in the evidence of Jake's help with the boat.

"You're short-handed, it seems to me," his grandson said. "Maria came into the fleet as manager-captain, but she brought her own boat, which"—he glanced at her—"she's still running, at least part-time. You've got an extra boat with no extra help."

"We're doin' fine with the help we got!"

Jake sucked in one cheek, glancing from Wyatt to Maria and back to his grandfather. She could sense him counting to ten.

Wyatt's fist banged down on the desk. "We were short one captain when you walked out on this fleet ten years ago too. But that didn't stop you then, did it?"

"Nothing would have stopped me then," was the grim reply.

"Well, then, what makes you think you can come waltzing back in here now and tell me how to run this business?"

"Wyatt," Maria said.

He glanced toward her, his arm raised for one more emphatic thump.

"I *am* the manager of this fleet," she told him before he could work himself into another tirade. "I was hired to handle problems like this so that you wouldn't have to worry about them."

Wyatt scowled at her.

His grandson regarded her with cool evaluation that sent quick shivers of emotion racing along her nerve endings. She didn't appreciate his coercive tactics, even in the face of Wyatt's admittedly unreasonable behavior. And she wasn't going to let herself become a pawn in his bid for information he couldn't ask for directly. If he wanted information on the fleet, he could get it for himself.

She lifted her chin and willed her voice to be steady. "Your grandson's right," she said. "We are short-handed. In two weeks we'll be flat out, with every boat on a full schedule." Her gaze met that of the former captain. "This would be a good time to hire someone temporarily."

Jake Marlow's face went blank, then he let out a

huff of disbelief and his mouth quirked at one corner. "You offering me the job?"

Wyatt drew in a breath that expanded his still-powerful chest. "The Marlow fleet doesn't need a man who walked out on it ten years ago!"

"Fine. The fleet won't get him. *I'll* offer you a temporary job," she told Jake, "working the *Spiritos*. My boat. She's small, she's fast, and she needs a captain." Her glance flicked back to her employer. "That way I'll be free to run one of the big boats if any of the captains is out, and it will give me the time I need to oversee the paperwork."

Wyatt sucked in one cheek, frowned at her, then jerked his chin toward his grandson.

"You think you could still handle a boat?" he challenged.

The challenge was returned. "I think maybe I could manage."

"Fine." Maria walked toward the desk. "We'll give it some discussion. But right now I'll call the house, before Mrs. Salintes has a nervous breakdown wondering where you are, Wyatt."

"Never mind!" the older man growled at her. "I'll walk back myself." He pushed himself out of the chair, strode to the door, then turned to give his grandson a scathing glance. "Just get it clear that you're not workin' for me!"

Jake watched him leave, then turned his gaze back to Maria. His gaze, steady on her face, held something she recognized.

She'd grown up in a world where a challenge from a woman to a man implied the kind of relationship where the woman had a claimant's right to issue challenges. She'd rejected that old, traditional view when she entered the working world, but under the touch of that hard, steady blue gaze, she couldn't deny the shiver that coursed through her at the thought of being this man's woman.

"I'll get us some coffee," she said abruptly, breaking the taut silence. "You can get used to vending-machine brew."

Two

What the hell had he agreed to?

Walking into the hallway and heading toward the customers' cafeteria, Jake pondered the question. When she opened the swinging door, he reached to hold it for her, as he had when they came in. She gave him a brief, neutral glance over her shoulder, then stepped into the room and crossed to the coffee machine. "Cream? Sugar?" she asked him.

"Black."

He let the door swing closed behind him.

She reached for a cardboard cup and fed quarters into the machine. The tail of her blue jersey reached past her hips, and with her every movement the knit fabric clung to the seat of her jeans and hinted at feminine curves beneath the layers of material. When she turned around, his eyes were at the level of her hips, and he let his gaze take plenty of time to reach her face.

Maria Santos had caught him off guard, from the moment she stepped out onto the deck of her boat and spoken to him. It wasn't part of his plan to work for the fleet, but then, he hadn't counted on Maria's idealistic sense of loyalty to his grandfather, or his own respect for that.

He hadn't counted on a lot of factors about Maria Santos, least of all his own explosive reaction to her. She left him feeling like he'd been hauled under the keel of a very elegant, seaworthy sailboat.

And as long as he came up on the other side, it might be worth getting wet.

"I'll take the job," he said softly.

She let out a quick breath. Something flickered in her eyes, sending a wave of heat coursing through his veins, then she blinked and straightened her shoulders. The moment was gone. She handed him the coffee. "Maybe you should try the vending-machine brew before you make that choice."

The brew smelled about the way he remembered it—bitter and overly strong. "I got used to vending-machine coffee a long time ago, Maria Santos."

"I know that, Mr. Marlow. What I don't know is why you feel the need to subject yourself to it again."

Jake studied her: the finely curved eyebrows over dark, almond-shaped eyes and a classically arched Mediterranean nose. She had the kind of smooth, golden skin that needed to be touched to be believed. Stroked very gently with the back of a knuckle or tasted with the tip of a tongue.

"Maybe I think you're right, Ms. Santos. If I want information about the fleet, I should get it firsthand. That's the gist of your message, right?"

She nodded, bringing her fingertips together around her cup in a curiously appealing gesture— Old World and introspective.

"You're not who I expected my grandfather to hire," he said.

"No? My credentials, as you've said yourself, are all in order."

"Oh, I know your credentials. M.S. in Marine Biology, minor in Business Administration, three years' experience running your own boat. I wasn't talking about your qualifications."

"Who did you think your grandfather would hire, then?"

"Someone he could order around."

Her mouth formed a silent "Ah," but she made no other comment.

"When did you get interested in whales?"

"I don't remember. I was always interested. I used to go on your grandfather's whale watches, back when he had the first boats in the harbor to do it. When you worked for him."

"Ten years ago."

"Longer than that. I envied you. I wanted your job."

He snorted in commentary. "You would have been a little young for it, I imagine."

"So were you." Without taking her eyes off him, she put her cup down on the counter behind her and faced him squarely, no barriers between them. "Mr. Marlow, I'm aware that you have a vested interest in the fleet and that the question of my competence is something you'd like to determine for yourself. I've hired you to captain the *Spiritos*, which I assume will tell you what you need to know."

"That's why you hired me?" he asked, wondering how much she'd guessed about what he needed to know.

"That and the fact that I don't want Wyatt upset."

"We have that in common, then. I don't want him upset either. And I think he'll be especially upset if something happens to the fleet while he's in forced retirement."

He watched a flare of color tint her cheeks. "It won't."

He nodded, then glanced down at the cup he held, swirling the coffee around. Wyatt obviously hadn't told her the whole history of Marlow Whale Watching. That didn't surprise him. Wyatt was far too unresigned to his temporary weakness to admit that the fleet might be in trouble and that he might need help. If Wyatt had told Maria of the recurrent "accidents" that had plagued Marlow Whale Watching in years past, she was too smart not to recognize the symptoms of sabotage. Either that or—he swirled the coffee again, fighting a sudden, unpleasant denial in the pit of his stomach—she was part of it.

She wasn't a likely candidate, either as a criminal or as someone's dupe. He believed, as he had when he'd read her reports, that she simply didn't guess the criminal possibilities of a few unlikely accidents. But he wasn't prepared to bet the Marlow fleet on it.

"Did you report any of these incidents to the police?"

She frowned. "No. That wasn't called for. None of the accidents involved another party."

He felt the beginnings of a grim smile that didn't quite reach his mouth. "And Wyatt didn't want any of this discussed at all, I'll bet. Least of all reported to the authorities."

For a moment she was silent. "Naturally he was upset by the idea of any kind of accident. He's spent his life worrying about the fleet and the welfare of his customers and his crews."

"My grandfather's spent his life worrying about his investments and antagonizing the people who work for him," Jake said bluntly.

She pushed herself away from the counter and turned aside, shaking her head. "Your grandfather might be a little difficult, Mr. Marlow, but—"

"And you might be a little naive, Ms. Santos." The comment was whiplash-sharp, and she responded to it the way he'd meant her to.

Her chin rose sharply, and the corners of her mouth tightened. "Why is that? Because I agree with policies that have made Wyatt one of the most successful captains in Gull Cove? Or because I find your grandfather more likable than you apparently can accept?"

He let out a breath through his teeth. "I doubt that you know him well enough to make an informed judgment."

"That's a harsh statement."

"We're a harsh family."

"Maybe so." It came out on a considering pause. "But I don't have any reason to believe your grandfather has been untruthful with me."

"Oh, he'd tell you his version of the truth, all right. It would be strongly edited, but that wouldn't bother him, because he's convinced he's always right."

She studied him for a moment, then, slowly, her mouth tipped up at the corners. It was the first smile he'd seen on her face, and he watched it curve her wide, generous mouth, aware of his own sensual reaction. She shook her head, denying his assertions in a way that should have annoyed him, but there was a hint of unexpected amusement in her eyes, a hint of laughter in her smile, that drew him like coffee on a cold morning. "He's not the only man in the world who tends to think he's always right," she said softly.

She was laughing at him, he realized. But he couldn't find in his own reaction a trace of anything but near-obsessive fascination. Her slow, unexpected smile sent liquid ripples all along his nerve endings.

"Obviously you get along with my grandfather better than most," he said finally.

"I have four brothers and a father who are all fishermen, like your grandfather was before he started the whale-watching business."

"Meaning they're all independent, egotistical, impossible to get along with, and stubborn as hell?"

"I wouldn't have put it quite that way."

How would she have put it? He swallowed a mouthful of hot, bitter coffee and let the harsh reality of vending-machine brew slide down his throat. What remained with him after he'd swallowed the coffee was a potent sensation of heat.

"No woman Wyatt's ever met has gotten him to stop swearing and sit down when he's told to," Jake said, watching her.

"Sitting down is in his best interest."

"Most of what he does is in his best interest."

She shook her head, releasing a slight, musical laugh. "You're very cynical, Mr. Marlow."

"I was raised by my grandfather."

She lifted her eyebrows and tilted her head back to consider him.

"You're going to tell me my grandfather's not a cynic?" he muttered.

"I think," she said, "he has a good heart. The cynicism is part of his act. It's possible to get beyond it, with a little tact."

Jake snorted. "I'd say it would take enough tact to fill the bay, but apparently you've got that. You're still working for him."

"So would you have been if you'd convinced him to hire you."

"I would've worked for the fleet, Ms. Santos. Not my grandfather."

She measured the reply with silence, then asked, "Will you work for me?"

He frowned.

"I won't have anyone running the *Spiritos* who doesn't answer directly to me, about the boat or the job."

The humming of the coffee machine was the only sound as he took in the statement. "I can run a boat," he said finally. "I can deal with customers, and I can turn a profit even competing with the fleet. I don't think you'll have any cause for complaint."

A flush of heat colored her face in a reaction he realized he'd been waiting for, anticipating. "I study whales, Mr. Marlow. I didn't go into this field to turn a profit. Yes, I do make money working for your grandfather. I have to support myself, I have to pay off the *Spiritos*, I'm hoping to finance a research trip this winter. But I don't cut costs, I don't endanger the whales for any reason—profit or schedule or curiosity—and I won't shortchange your grandfather for my own personal goals."

Her voice had risen as she talked, and her hands had tightened around the edge of the counter. He was subtly aware of the tension in her body, the way she leaned toward him, arguing what she believed with an underlying passion more convincing than mere words.

"I hope he appreciates your loyalty."

She blinked. "Is that sarcasm?"

"No." Jake recognized the gruff quality of his own voice with another level of sensual awareness. "It's rivalry."

A potent image rose in his mind, like water flowing over smooth stones, of slim, supple strength and sweet, willing surrender. If he touched her, slid his fingers along her waist, cupped his palm around the curve of her hip, would her skin feel as resilient and supple as he imagined? Strong and soft together, like a spring wind in front of a storm.

She cleared her throat. "You haven't really answered my question, Mr. Marlow." There was a husky, breathless quality to her voice that stroked every masculine nerve ending in his body.

"It's Jake," he said.

She nodded, but didn't say his name.

"You're very serious, aren't you?"

She blinked. "Serious?"

"You hardly smile. You don't laugh."

"We haven't been talking about humorous subjects." But her mouth curved slightly.

"Maybe we could try it," he suggested.

"I beg your pardon?"

"Humorous subjects." He gestured with his cup. "Lousy coffee. Sea gulls. Off-color jokes."

She smiled again, and gave a self-conscious shrug of her shoulders. "I'm afraid I can't think of any at the moment."

"Funny," he said, looking at her, "neither can I."

"I have work to do, Mr. Marlow. I should get to it."

He waited until she'd poured her coffee into the sink and turned back to face him before he spoke. "There is still the question of whether we can work together."

She started to say something, but the words caught in her throat, and he watched, mesmerized, as her tongue flicked out to moisten her lips. She swallowed, nodding.

Maria Santos, of the cool, competent manner and translucent skin and lithe grace, had given the slightest, most reluctant signal that she wanted him, and Jake was shaken to the core of his being.

The realization swept through him with the force of a tidal wave. He'd wanted women before, but not with the gut-level, elemental need that this woman aroused with just a tentative glance from her young-ancient eyes and the barest shiver of her strong and fragile body. She made him feel things he thought he'd deadened with too much hard experience. It wasn't so. He wanted her the way sailors three thousand years ago had wanted the sirens who sang to them from the rocks, the way mythic mariners had wanted their sea sprites half a world away. And whatever the appropriate reaction of the moment, he couldn't stop himself from touching her now.

"I think," he murmured, "it's definitely worth a try." He reached for her, pulled her against him, and brought his head down to meet her mouth.

Maria gasped in surprise as Jake Marlow's mouth covered hers in a kiss that could have made her forget her own name. The concrete floor spun beneath her feet. She put her hands on his shoulders and clung to him as the reality of the cafeteria disappeared and Jake's hard, muscular body replaced it. For an inexplicable moment her mouth opened under his, and all she wanted was time and privacy and Jake's body pressed against hers so closely, there were no spaces and no words and no denials.

When he lifted his head and drew back, the pulse in the hollow of his throat was racing, and the blatant impatience of his body against hers was impossible to ignore. She felt his hands thread into her hair, and he tipped her head up toward his. There was a question in his eyes.

She met his gaze for a moment while the world, piece by piece, settled back into place. The realization that Jake Marlow was asking her a question she should never have invited sank into her consciousness, treacherously late.

She flattened her palms on his arms, pushing herself away from him, and kept pushing until she felt his hands loosen on her back and she could step away.

He was frowning slightly, eyebrows drawn together as he searched her face. She read puzzlement, confusion, and hot, undisguised hunger in his gaze. He had a right to all of them . . . and she never should have given that right.

"No," she said, the word husky with her own emotions, but unmistakably clear.

He stared at her a moment longer, his breathing still rapid. Then without another word he combed his fingers through the thatch of blond hair that had fallen over his forehead and walked out of the cafeteria.

It was close to dark by the time Maria left the office, pulled the heavy metal door shut behind her, and leaned back against it, cradling her thermos in both hands. It had taken her three hours to finish the routine paper work. The three big Marlow boats were all back in their slips, empty of customers, secured and battened down for the night.

A strident gull wheeled along the length of the dock toward the *Spiritos*. Maria pushed herself away from the door and headed toward her boat.

"Maria!" From the pilot house of the *Dolphin* Miguel, its captain, waved to her, his stocky figure dim against the pilot house doorway.

She leaned out from one of the pilings and called up to him. "You're still on board?"

"The caterer just left."

"This late?"

"He said he had to stock all the ships' galleys. Everyone was low. Watching whales is hungry work."

She laughed. "I thought you were living on love these days, cousin."

His grin was a slash of white in the growing darkness. "Love conquers all except hunger. And anyway, Lucy's a good cook. She needs an appreciative appetite, doesn't she?"

"I guess she's found one. Say hello to her for me when you see her."

"Maria?" She turned back again. "What happened, with the argument? With Marlow, this afternoon."

She should have known he'd ask. The whole harbor had no doubt heard Wyatt's ranting. Someone was sure to have pieced the facts together and spread the gossip. "Jake Marlow is taking a little time off from the insurance business," she told Miguel. "He wants to work the fleet. I hired him on as captain of the *Spiritos*."

There was a pause. "Jake Marlow?" Miguel said. "The old man's grandson?" For a moment his dark figure went still, then he shrugged, made a noncommittal sound, and waved before turning back into the pilothouse.

Maria wrapped her hands around the thermos bottle, watching for a moment as the *Dolphin* thudded almost soundlessly against the rubber bumpers that protected her hull. Beside her, from the deck of the *Harbor Seal*, the tinny whir of a vacuum cleaner announced the presence of the maintenance crew, who'd been put on extra hours after the power loss in that boat's galley. On the dock in front of both boats glowing red lights indicated that the security system was in service.

Maria turned toward the *Spiritos* and walked on, her sneakers squeaking on the dock, her gaze scanning the dark harbor, where the lights of Gull Point twinkled distantly toward the open ocean.

She didn't have to spell out the fact that Jake Marlow was checking on his investment and that they would all, herself especially, have to submit to being graded. It wouldn't go down with the captains any more easily than it did with her. The unspoken rules of business were that Jake Marlow should trust his grandfather's judgment and, by extension, hers.

But Jake Marlow, she thought, didn't have much trust left in him. And the complications that caused made her head ache just thinking about them.

She was willing to allow that Jake had a right to be concerned with the bottom line. He had a legitimate interest. And because it was her job, she'd deal with it.

That didn't mean she wanted to kiss it.

She shut her eyes for a moment, taking in a deep breath, too aware of the shiver of response at the memory of his kiss. *Mae de Deus.* What was the matter with her?

A wet breeze was coming in off the water. The bell buoy clanged twice. Out in the channel a forty-five-foot trawler was making its way into the harbor. She watched, wondering what the catch had been like, imagining for a moment the boat's welcome at dock, the smells of diesel fuel and salt water and fish, the men shouting in satisfaction or complaint about the catch. In her imagined scene there was no woman. In her family, men fished, women kept house.

"Never saw a girl so crazy about fishing," her mother had been apt to say about Maria. "You'll marry a fisherman, and spend your life worrying about him."

She hadn't wanted to marry one, though. She'd wanted to be one. She'd wanted to make her living on the water, surrounded by the smell and the sound and the ancient rhythm of the sea. And, against all odds, she'd done it. The loan on *Spiritos* was half paid off in the three years of private whale-watching charters she had run. When Wyatt Marlow had needed a manager, he'd come directly to the woman he described as his stiffest competition. She'd achieved her present success by single-minded concentration on her goals. Her first love was the sea; her second, her studies; and her third, the *Spiritos.*

Her life had no room for any other entanglements.

She made her way down the ramp to the catwalk beside *Spiritos.* Without bothering with the gangplank, she leaned over the water to grasp the railing and jumped. The boat shifted slowly as she landed. She made her way across the deck and opened the door to the small cabin.

"Welcome aboard, Captain," Jake Marlow said.

Three

He stood up as she walked in, pushing his hands into his pockets, shifting his weight to one hip. She became still for a moment, absorbing the fact of Jake Marlow in her cabin, then flicked on the lights and let the door swing shut. He'd changed to jeans and a faded cotton sweater, the hem hooked over something in the back pocket of his jeans. He turned to gesture at the bunk where he'd been sitting, and she caught the glint of a tarnished metal cylinder protruding from the threadbare pocket.

"You weren't here when I walked down," he said. "So rather than skulking around the docks like a prowler, I broke in."

"So I see." She set the thermos down on a counter. The cylinder was a tarnished metal spyglass small enough to be a child's toy, picked up and perhaps stuffed distractedly into a pocket. She wondered if he knew he had it. "Did you run up the skull and crossbones?" she asked him.

He laughed, the sound husky, low, and masculine. "I didn't dare," he said. "I was afraid as captain I might be forced to walk the plank."

"You're in a tough position," she agreed. "As a captain you'll walk the plank and as a pirate you'll probably end up being hung."

"Only if I get caught. And even then only if the lady who owns the ship presses charges."

She gave him a short, level appraisal and raised her eyebrows. "That's what you're counting on to save you from the noose?"

"Counting on? No." His glance rested on her for a moment, then the corners of his mouth curled up. "But it's certainly one possibility."

It certainly was. She swore to herself again in Portuguese. It was all too easy to imagine Jake Marlow, Wall Street pirate, being saved from the noose because the woman he'd just kissed refused to press charges. She turned away from him to reach for a mug from the locker above the counter. "You could try sticking to the rules," she said lightly.

His glance flicked to her hands holding the mug, then to her mouth, and his voice roughened almost imperceptibly. "I usually do. With a few lapses, I go more for gentle persuasion than force."

She'd been right to think of him as a pirate, she realized, registering again the unexpectedly sensual response Jake Marlow had on her thoughts. He was dangerous. He could topple her equilibrium before she knew what was happening, if she let him, and force would be entirely unnecessary. " 'Gentle persuasion' isn't what it sounded like when you and your grandfather confronted each other this afternoon."

He met her gaze, serious for a moment, then the Marlow smile turned up one corner of his mouth. "I know," he said unexpectedly. "I didn't mean to get him stirred up this afternoon, but old habits . . ." His mouth thinned. "And I have a hell of a time believing he's not invincible."

She put the mug down on the table, then reached for another one. She could understand, in part, the need to believe Wyatt invincible. "His doctors say in another month he might be able to go back to work part-time."

"I know that. I've talked to them. Every day since he was admitted as a matter of fact."

"Every day?"

"One of them is a personal friend of mine."

"I see." She digested that information. It put Jake in a new light, but one that didn't surprise her. Beneath his facade of cynicism he had impulses that contradicted it. She wondered if he realized it. "And did you *ask* this friend to take your grandfather on as a patient?"

"Yes. He's one of the best cardiologists in his field. My grandfather wasn't in a position to argue. He had a serious problem. I don't leave things like that to chance."

"Something tells me you leave very little to chance," she said wryly.

He shrugged. "It's not good business."

She smiled. "And—of course—you would approach your grandfather's illness as a business problem."

"The approach worked."

She smiled again and withheld comment.

Jake's mouth quirked at the corners. "In insurance, Ms. Santos, *chance* is the word we use for a casualty that probably should have been prevented."

Her head tipped to one side, she said, "Like your grandfather's heart attack?"

He shrugged. "Like my grandfather's next heart attack. With the right precautions it can probably be prevented."

"Yes, we can hope so." She paused a moment, and her eyes flicked to the child's toy sticking out of his back pocket. "Are you staying at the house?"

"He offered me my old room." His smile was wry. "The better to keep tabs on me, I assume."

"Yes, you would assume that. Do you always make the cynical assumption?"

"The reasonable assumption, Ms. Santos. And yes, I come to conclusions based on reasonable assumptions. You're a businesswoman. I'm sure you do the same."

She considered a moment. "I leave some place for instinct."

"*Instinct.*" He shook his head. "That's not a word the Marlows put a lot of faith in."

She regarded him in silence, and he returned the look, his eyes narrowed. "It isn't a word we like in the insurance business either."

She unscrewed the cap to the thermos and poured tea into the mugs. She offered one to Jake, and when he took it, she asked, "Are we talking about your grandfather, Mr. Marlow, or are we talking about the way I manage the fleet?"

He shrugged, ignoring the challenge in her question, but apparently at ease with the change of subject. "I noticed the new security system on the boats. That's your doing, I presume."

"Yes. I think it's a good idea to update security from time to time."

He watched her a moment. "When did you decide that?"

"Shortly after I took over management of the business. I believe in . . . insurance." She picked up her mug and turned to face him, leaning back against the small table. "But there's more to whale watching than business, Mr. Marlow. Customers come on whale watches because they want that rare experience of contact with another species, another kind of intelligence. I take reasonable precautions for security, I know what my employees are doing, and beyond that I trust my instincts. I have to. There are some things about this business that can't be understood any other way."

"Like what?" he asked, obviously curious.

"The intelligence of humpback whales."

Outside the small cabin, water lapped against the hull of the *Spiritos* while Jake said nothing for a minute. Then he gestured at her with his mug. "You take your whales very seriously, don't you, Ms. Santos?"

It was the second time he'd accused her of being overly serious. Under his amused appraisal, Maria had to stop herself from snapping out some awkward, defensive protest that she did indeed have a sense of humor.

To her consternation, though, she couldn't quite manage a dignified silence. She said, a little testily, "As one of the owners of Marlow Whale Watching, I would have thought that would please you."

"I would have thought so too." He glanced down at his tea, but didn't lift the mug to his lips. "You know, I came here to apologize—to say I was out of line this afternoon. I had no business kissing you, and I had no intention of compromising a clear-cut business relationship."

The rough edge to his voice did funny things to her throat. She swallowed and—this time—said nothing.

"I was going to tell you I didn't know what got into me." He chuckled and grinned at her. "Then you walked in here . . . and it occurred to me that would be a ridiculous thing to say. I know damn well what got into me."

She drew in a sharp breath. "It's not necessary to say anything. Really. As a matter of fact, it's not necessary to apologize. Sometimes those things happen, but . . ." She realized she was babbling and made herself stop. "I'm sure it won't happen again," she said finally.

"Why not?"

"I . . . beg your pardon?"

"I said, why not?"

She filled her lungs with a badly needed breath of air, taken aback by the candid roughness in his tone. Just what did he expect her to say? "You work for me, Mr. Marlow. I'm your boss. Or you're mine, considering that you own thirty percent of the Marlow fleet. And we both know you're here to check me out as a manager. I think that makes things complicated enough for now."

He shrugged, making a dismissive gesture with his tea mug that relegated her argument to un-importance. "I'm here to check out the business, that's true. But it doesn't necessarily mean we're on opposite sides of—"

"I take my work seriously, Mr. Marlow," she said more forcefully. "As you've pointed out. This isn't just a casual job to me. I have a career to establish, this boat to pay off. . . ."

His pirate's gaze held her eyes with interest and assessment, letting her finish.

" . . . And I'm not looking for a new relationship right now."

He was silent, absorbing what she'd said, but his eyes didn't waver from her face. "Is there an old relationship? Someone you're committed to?"

The answer was no, but she didn't want to admit it. Not with Jake Marlow's interested, probing gaze fixed on her. "Yes. As a matter of fact there is."

There was another moment's silence. Jake's fingers tightened around his mug, then he asked softly, "Anyone I know?"

The determination in the question astonished her. What made him think he could ask her something so personal? Or that she'd answer? Or, for that matter, that he had a right to walk onto her boat without permission, take back his apology before he made it, and then make her feel grim and humorless and impossibly awkward because she took her work seriously!

She let out a long breath, calculating a suitable response to his overly personal question. On a spark of instant impulse she said casually, "You'll probably know him soon enough. His name is Joaquim."

"Joaquim? He works with you?"

There was enough gruff antagonism in his voice to make the corners of her mouth twitch. She nodded. "He comes around almost every day, and he's hard to miss. He weighs around fifty tons."

Jake blinked, his fist still gripping the mug, then said deadpan, "A whale. You're involved with a whale."

"Oh, yes. Emotionally as well as on a . . . business level." She grinned. "It has its rewards."

"I'll take your word for it." He took his first sip of the tea, then smiled back at her and raised the cup in acknowledgment that she'd gotten him.

The good humor was appealing, and she considered it for a moment, trying to reconcile the disparate aspects of Jake's character. "You never got attached to any of the whales when you were whale watching?"

He lifted his gaze to the deck above them, considering, then shook his head. "No."

"You missed the best part of it, then."

He nodded, then frowned at her, mock-serious. "Anyone ever tell you the problems you can expect in one of these interspecies relationships? You know how many of them end up in counseling?"

She laughed. "Maybe I believe love conquers all."

He smiled again, but there was a hard edge to the expression. "Maybe you've never been to a divorce court."

The half-serious answer put her at a loss. She thought they'd been kidding, but somehow she'd touched a nerve, and she didn't quite know what to say. "No," she admitted. "I've never been to a divorce court."

A flicker of bitterness, tempered perhaps with regret for ill-considered words, came and went in his flint-blue eyes. He skated over the moment with a brisk gesture that cut off the subject of divorce, and, to her relief, any further discussion of possible relationships. "So. When do I get to meet this Joaquim? If I'm going to captain this tub, you'd better show me the ropes. I'm free whenever you are."

"So you are," she said, matching his tone. "But the *Spiritos* isn't. Tomorrow's the only day she isn't booked, so we'd better make it then."

"Name your hour, Captain." He grinned at her. "Or is *Captain* inaccurate now that I'm scheduled to take over?"

She raised her eyebrows at him, smiling. "Most of the crew call me *Boss*."

"Do they, now?"

"And the *Spiritos* isn't 'this tub.' She may be worth a tenth what one of the fleet boats cost, but she's mine, and I mortgaged my soul to buy her. So show a little respect, Marlow."

"Got it."

"Ten-thirty," she said dismissively. "High tide tomorrow morning."

He took the hint gracefully, setting his mug on the table and moving toward the door. "I'll be there."

"Good."

"Oh, and Maria?" he said, one hand on the door, his shoulder almost touching hers.

She glanced up at him, her heart beating a little faster at the slow, caressing way he said her name.

"I'll bring the skull and crossbones. Anybody who has a relationship with a whale has to have a latent sense of adventure."

"You're courting the noose, Captain," she told him, but her voice was a little too husky.

His grin was three parts impudence and one part promise. "I'll chance it," he said. The door shut behind him, his footsteps crossed the deck, then the *Spiritos* swayed as he jumped from the deck.

Still holding her tea mug, Maria stared at the door, listening to her heart beating with unmistakable sensual anticipation, and reminding herself of all the good reasons why a relationship with Jake Marlow wouldn't work. Not the least of which was that she could imagine that damn skull and crossbones in Jake Marlow's strong and determined hands, backed by a rakish grin and the unshakable belief that anything he wanted he could leap onto the deck and take, probably sweeping it off its usually sensible feet into an eighteenth-century swoon.

Exasperated with herself, she crossed the small cabin to the galley and dumped the remains of Jake's tea into the sink.

She'd been kissed before. She knew what sexual attraction was. It hadn't been *that* long.

Even if it had, Jake Marlow was not the man to end her abstinence with. He was her employee, an owner of the company, and her boss's grandson. And she wasn't crazy enough to get involved with him.

Her face composed into an expression of determination, she took a sip of tea, stared into her cup, then, in another exasperated move, dumped the rest of it down the sink.

In the back bedroom of his grandfather's house, Jake stood at the window looking out at the boat Maria Santos had hired him to run, toying with the old spyglass he'd been carrying around since he'd found it there. He smiled a little as he resisted the urge to train the spyglass on Maria's cabin and hope she was waltzing around in the kind of black lacy thing he'd been imagining she wore under her fisherman's jersey.

He couldn't remember the last time he'd been so drawn to a woman. Or the last time he'd kissed one with so little provocation. But the thought of her brief, warm response brought a visceral satisfaction he could feel, even two hundred yards away from her, in the hardening of his body and the increased rhythm of his heartbeat. Her mouth opening to his, the curve of her supple, graceful back as she'd leaned against him, the brief warmth and softness of her breasts against his chest before she'd pushed herself away and said *No* in that soft, precise accent that fascinated him a hell of a lot more than the word.

No was far too final for what she did to his hormonal system. Not to mention his . . . judgment, he decided with wry humor. Any man who'd felt a moment of jealousy toward a whale was already in deep water.

He glanced out at the *Spiritos* again, his smile fading as he considered Maria's passionate dedication to her whales, her loyalty to Wyatt, her straightforward dealings with the insurance claims. His instincts told him she was honest, and it pricked his conscience that he couldn't be honest himself.

But dammit, he'd witnessed enough insurance investigations to know you didn't conduct them by charging in and announcing your presence. And his own personal history told him just how much he could trust his own instincts. His ex-wife, Jeanine, and an expensive divorce settlement had long since disenchanted him of the notion of instinctive trust. You could trust people to have their own personal needs: companionship, sex, mutually shared advantage, if you were lucky. He was willing to grant that much. Going any further than that was foolhardy.

A light flicked on and off on the *Porpoise,* and Jake's gaze moved to the big boat. Maria had established a policy of requiring the captains to be on board whenever the boats were being supplied, cleaned, or maintained. It was a good policy, Jake thought, setting up a clear line of responsibility for the boats, and—incidentally—making any kind of sabotage difficult.

Difficult, but not impossible. There'd be another "accident." The question was when. And who.

Evidence pointed to one of the captains, either directly or as a dupe. And that short list had to include Maria herself.

Jake pursed his lips in a silent whistle and snapped the spyglass against his palm, wondering what anyone would learn by spying on Maria Santos. She wasn't the target he'd choose if he had criminal designs on the fleet of boats she managed. She was too gutsy, too smart, and too loyal to be easily bribed or used. And, he admitted, the thought of Maria being used for someone else's purposes did things to his gut that had too much to do with instinct.

He wasn't going to let himself trust the Marlow fleet to that kind of instinct. Maria, whether he wanted to face it or not, cared about her whales with enough passion to make her—possibly— vulnerable to someone who knew how to use that. She had a blind spot that wasn't shared by the kind of tough, ruthless ambition Jake knew about firsthand.

If it came down to Maria's love for her whales or the economic interests of Marlow Whale Watching, Jake knew what side he'd have to take.

The whales wouldn't win.

Four

The perfect weather held over to the next day. The morning was bright and windless, the harbor so smooth it gleamed, when Maria stepped out on deck to check bowline and bumpers. She pushed up the sleeves of her shirt, shaded her eyes, and peered out toward the mouth of the harbor. Miguel was already out with the *Dolphin,* and the *Porpoise* was scheduled to go at noon. Over Stellwagon Bank humpbacks would be feeding. Maria swallowed a sound of impatience, wishing she'd told Jake Marlow to meet her earlier.

She needn't have bothered. When she turned toward the dock, he was jumping down from the seawall, walking along the dock toward the *Spiritos* wearing snug jeans and a faded blue sweater that draped his broad shoulders with familiarity and hinted of hard, honed muscles underneath it. A windbreaker was hooked on a finger over one shoulder.

She watched him, half mesmerized, her hand still shading her eyes though the sun was at her back, until he ambled to a stop on the catwalk in front of her. His glance lingered for a moment. Her flannel shirt and cutoff jeans didn't reveal much, she knew, but she doubted Jake's imagination needed much help. Nor did *hers*, she admitted.

"Morning." The deep, masculine drawl set up some kind of sympathetic vibration in the deepest part of her midsection.

She dropped her hand, self-consciously tucking it into her pocket. "Good morning, Captain Marlow. You're here early."

"I had a feeling you'd be eager to get going." He grinned, rocking a little on the balls of his feet. His hair, blond in the sunlight, fell over his forehead with boyish innocence. He balled up his windbreaker and tossed first it, then his duffel up onto the deck at her feet. His grin when she hopped back out of the way should have been banned by truth-in-advertising laws. "I didn't want you to leave without me."

"I *was* considering it," she told him. "The *Dolphin*'s been out an hour and a half, and Miguel's already spotted a whale. I was wishing I'd told you to get here earlier."

He glanced toward the *Dolphin*'s empty slip, then looked back at her. "Yeah?" he said, his voice husky, managing to sound suggestive even with a deck and half a catwalk between them. "So you were waiting impatiently for me, huh?"

It was almost impossible to suppress an answering smile to that pirate's grin. Flustered that she couldn't quite hide her reaction, Maria bent to pick up the duffel and jacket and tucked them both under her arm. "As long as you're here, I'll fire up the engine, and you can cast off."

"Sure." He glanced at the lines securing the boat, then looked back at her. "Hey, go easy on that duffel, will you?"

She loosened her hold on it, frowning. "What's in it?"

"Lunch." He grinned again. "Loaf of bread, jug of wine, skull and crossbones . . ."

She took in a long breath, giving the duffel a wry appraisal. He'd brought everything he needed for seduction or ravishment, had he? She gave him a level glance, eyebrows raised. "Lunch is on me, Captain," she told him. "*Provided* you do a satisfactory morning's work." She stepped into the wheelhouse, ignoring whatever answer he chose to give, and dropped his things on the deck. Automatically she checked all the gauges on the console before she fired up the twin diesels that powered the *Spiritos*.

She listened for a moment to the smooth, steady rumble of the engines, feeling familiar vibrations through the hull. For three years *Spiritos* had taken her wherever she wanted to go. She could do twenty knots in any seas she happened to encounter and run as steady and smooth as a liner twice her size. She felt a sudden, proprietary reluctance at the thought of putting *Spiritos* in someone else's hands. She knew Jake had the experience to pilot a boat. But . . . *her* boat?

She leaned to poke her head out the wheelhouse door. "Cast off!" she ordered.

Jake bent to the lines, uncoiled and heaved them on deck, then, with an easy leap, followed them onto the boat.

His steps crossed the deck, then his long body blocked the light as he leaned against the doorjamb, taking in the small, enclosed space, watching her as she stood at the wheel. Backlit from the doorway, his eyes were a deeper blue than they had looked in her cabin the night before, but the frank, masculine interest in his gaze was every bit as unsettling. She had a quick, sharp certainty that if he kissed her, he would taste like coffee.

When she didn't move, he frowned. "Are you going to take her out?"

"No." She shook her head. "You are."

He glanced toward the wheel and the console full of gauges, shrugged, then grinned at her. "Okay."

She stepped out of his way, and he took her place. He ran his fingers over the gauges just as she had, then looked around the small wheelhouse with curiosity and no apparent uneasiness. His appraisal stopped at the gear she had stacked in the corner. "What's that?" he asked.

"A hydrophone. An underwater microphone basically."

"To listen to the whales?"

"Yes."

He frowned. "I thought they only sang in the winter, down south. That it was mating behavior, or something."

"I don't think anyone knows what kind of behavior it is, but"—she crossed her arms in front of her, self-conscious—"it's true, most biologists believe they sing only in their winter grounds."

"*Most* biologists?"

She shrugged. "There are a lot of things we don't know yet about whales."

He acknowledged her statement with the raising of one eyebrow, but, to her relief, didn't pursue her unorthodox theories about where and when the whales sang.

He turned his attention to the boat, checked the console once again, and shifted one engine into reverse. Maria bit back the urge to talk him through the undocking. Clearly he hadn't expected instructions. He backed the *Spiritos* cleanly away from her slip, then, with not so much as a glance in Maria's direction, maneuvered her around toward open water and set her on a course toward the mouth of the harbor as if he'd done it every day of his life.

When they were under way, he grinned at her. "Do I pass muster, boss?"

"I don't think you really have to ask." *Or have to have such a sexy grin.* To keep herself from grinning back, she said, "You can cut across the end of the point this close to high t—"

"I know."

He'd already altered their course, adjusting so automatically to the tides and the idiosyncrasies of Gull Cove Harbor that she hadn't noticed him doing it. She laughed, loosening her shoulders and crossing her arms in front of her chest. "You don't seem to be having any trouble remembering your seamanship."

"Yeah, well, it's not something you forget, is it?"

"I wouldn't know. I've never been away from it long enough."

He studied her a moment. "A sea spirit, are you?" he murmured. "Well, there was a time when I couldn't imagine being away from it that long either."

She heard something almost wishful in his voice beneath the brisk, matter-of-fact comment—a note of vulnerability that contrasted with his cynical humor and ruthlessly businesslike philosophy. Caught by it, she uncrossed her arms and pushed her hands into her pockets. "So . . . why'd you leave?"

"My grandfather and I had a falling out." His mouth twitched at one corner. "Don't tell me you haven't heard the story."

"I've heard it. But you could have stayed closer to home than you did. You could have started your own whale-watching business, for that matter."

"Uh-uh." He shook his head. "One ocean wasn't big enough for the two of us."

Beneath their feet *Spiritos* glided smoothly through the waveless surface of the harbor, her engines steady, the sound now obscured by familiarity and the soft swish of water across her hull. "It's hard for me to imagine that," she said finally. "The ocean seems so immense . . . so infinite. Hard to imagine there wouldn't be room for grandfather and grandson."

"That's the way you see it? An ocean big enough to encompass all viewpoints?"

"Something like that."

"Well, I suppose it depends on what end of the spyglass you're looking through, doesn't it?"

It took her a moment to get the reference, then she shook her head, smiling. "Did your grandfather give you that spyglass?"

"Yes. He did. Taught me how to use it too."

"I thought he might have."

He gave a single huff of laughter, but the sound held no warmth. "Don't sentimentalize my grandfather, Sea Sprite." His hand tightened on the wheel. "Or me," he added, almost under his breath. The pause before the last two words made them sound like a stark, cryptic warning.

She frowned. Had he meant them that way? For the space of a few heartbeats she went still, and a shiver of apprehension worked its way up her spine. She had a brief sense of what it had cost him to ally himself with his grandfather, even in those two words.

Mae de Deus. Her own cautions echoed in her mind, not quite dismissible. "Or *you*?" she repeated. "Are you giving me fair warning, Jake Marlow?"

He returned her look with the flint-blue gaze of a true Marlow. When she didn't move or speak, he shrugged and muttered, "No, Sea Sprite. Commenting on your naïveté."

At her frown he shrugged again, and his face relaxed into the easy grin that so charmed her. "I *already* warned you about me. Yesterday."

Discomposed by the quick switch, she murmured, "Yesterday?"

His gaze flicked to her mouth and lingered suggestively. When he looked up, his eyes, once again, held charming mischief. "I'll do it again if you like."

"No, you won't," she snapped. "Not while you're supposed to be at the helm of my boat."

She half expected him to laugh outright at the odd retort—the first thing she'd thought of—but he subdued his reaction to teasing amusement. "No," he agreed. "Not while I've got my hands on your boat. But you did mention . . . lunch, if I recall."

She recalled. She'd said it was *on her*. To her discomfort the memory of that unfortunate phrasing sent a wave of heat to her face . . . and precisely the wrong message to the man piloting her boat with a smug grin and a pirate's intentions. He was staring at her, fascinated, as if he'd never seen a woman blush before.

"Look, Mr. Marlow . . ."

"If you're about to reprimand me for my out-of-line thoughts," he muttered wryly, "you could at least call me Jake."

"Jake, then. What I mentioned was a morning's work and a whale watcher's lunch. And I think I've had all the warnings I need."

"You sure, Sea Sprite?" His expression sobered, and his voice turned husky. "I haven't been out on the water in three years. And there's no one I can think of I'd rather be out here with than you. That's the simple truth, Maria. It has nothing to do with who works for who."

A rush of heady possibilities whispered at the edges of her imagination. The words were too true to contradict. Maria felt her pulse beat faster, and a tingling at the back of her neck gave warning to the far-too-vulnerable threads of her common sense. "I'm not going to . . . flirt with you, Jake. It's not a good idea."

"I wasn't flirting."

She glanced toward the dappled surface of the water beyond the mouth of the harbor, then dropped her gaze to the control panel in front of Jake. "The only reason you're here, no matter how you put it, is because you need to know whether I'm capable of handling your investment in this business."

He let out a breath. "Maria, that's not the—"

"Yes," she said deliberately. "It is. I'm responsible for this fleet and everything that goes on in it. If some employee's been negligent, I'm responsible for letting that happen. If there's been a lack of precautions, I'm to blame. I'm not summer help, Jake." Her voice dropped to a low but determined murmur that held some emotion much deeper than threatened competence. "And I don't want a two-week fling with the boss's grandson."

For a moment his gaze was so intense, she felt it down to the pit of her stomach.

It was a put-down he didn't deserve, and she knew it. Jake was no spoiled boss's brat. He'd earned all the privileges he'd ever had from Wyatt, even when as a teenager he'd worked his way up to captain. For a moment regret churned in her stomach, and the realization of how much it affected her wrapped a band of panic around her chest. If anything happened between them, Jake Marlow would be no two-week fling. Not for her.

He shut his eyes, breaking off the wordless communication, tipped his head back, and ran a hand through his hair. He whistled through his teeth, long enough to make it obvious he'd learned the imitation singing teapot as a preadolescent, then grinned at her. "How about a two-week fling with the new captain?" he asked.

Relief at the dissolving tension freed her voice. "What do you expect me to say to that?"

"What do I expect? I expect you're going to tell me no and change the subject to whales. That's what you always do. And maybe you'll threaten me with Joaquim."

She smiled. "We *are* out here looking for whales. And Joaquim *will* be here."

"You're sure of that."

"Oh, yes."

"Oh, yes," he echoed ironically. "Your *instincts*, huh?"

"You'd better start honing your own instincts if you want to follow whales, Captain Marlow."

He shook his head. "I doubt we've got any of the same ones, Boss. And if mine were any more honed, I'd be challenging Joaquim to a duel." He grinned mischievously. "And he outweighs me by forty-nine point nine tons."

She covered her eyes with one hand and shook her head, but laughter made a delicious bubble catch in her throat. He wasn't any cold, bitter cynic out for whatever he could get, with no soul to lose. And despite his own warnings he wasn't his grandfather. His brand of charm and male interest was irresistible, and the rare glimpses he gave of his inner self pulled at her heart like the tide.

It would take all her effort to remember she *was* boss. If her own treacherous reactions were anything to go by, forty-nine point nine tons wasn't nearly enough to keep her out of Jake Marlow's arms.

Jake kept the *Spiritos* steady at eighteen knots, straight on her course toward Stellwagon Bank, the rich oceanic feeding grounds for so many species of marine life off the coast of Massachusetts. The *Spiritos*, as neat and steady a craft as he'd ever piloted, required little of his attention, though he doubted Maria would have let him bring her boat to any harm.

It was an hour's run, and as they approached the Bank, she checked with the other whale watchers on radio. Miguel broke in before she'd finished.

"Got another one, *Spiritos*," came the static-edged greeting.

"Good work, *Dolphin*," Maria told him. "Who have you got?"

"Couldn't tell. We're following. He's headed toward the others. Most of the sightings are south of here."

"Right. Let me know when you've got an ID." She set the microphone back in its bracket and reached for the binoculars hanging by their strap above the console.

Jake glanced at the compass and made a correction in their course. "We're heading south, Boss?" he asked her.

She turned the binoculars southward, then scanned the empty horizon around them, frowning. "No," she said suddenly. "Cut the power. We'll stay here for a while."

"Here? But there aren't any whales here."

"So far."

He hesitated over the console, and she grinned at him, looking impish and amused. "What's the matter, Captain? You don't trust my instincts?"

He saluted her with two fingers and cut the engines. In the ensuing silence the *Spiritos* settled in a liquid hiss of wake.

"You've got binoculars in your pack?" she asked.

He nodded.

"Well, get them out, then." She'd already stepped toward the door. "I'll get us a couple of sandwiches. You want a soda?"

"Sure," he said to her retreating back as she headed toward the galley. Amused at her illogical decision, he reached for his pack, got out the binoculars, and stepped out on deck.

All around them the blue Atlantic stretched calm and smooth, rippled by only a faint breeze. A distant fishing boat was the only other human sign. Behind the *Spiritos* a jaeger wheeled and dove, then, as the last of their churning wake dissolved, the bird tipped its pointed wings and glided away.

Jake pursed his lips in a silent whistle, wondering for a moment at the remote possibility that their position might be precarious. They were a single boat on a big ocean. Anyone with a dark motive, and an interest in getting rid of Wyatt's top-notch manager, could have sabotaged the *Spiritos* in the same ways the other Marlow boats may have been sabotaged. The accidents to the fleet had, so far, been minor, but there was no guarantee they would remain so, or that Maria's boat would be excluded from the possibilities of damage. Her radio, her engines . . . her hull, for that matter. The *Spiritos* wasn't protected by the new security system. Yet.

"Ginger ale okay?" Maria let the door to the galley swing shut behind her and crossed the deck toward him, balancing sodas, sandwiches, and an armful of electronic equipment. He recognized the hydrophone, and was surprised to realize he felt a lift of curiosity, despite his logical reservations about the possibility of hearing whales.

"Yes. Ginger ale's fine," he said.

She handed him the can of soda and a plastic-wrapped sandwich, then set her own lunch down on the deck. Leaning over the railing, she unhooked the metal rod that held the hydrophone. With the efficiency of long practice, she threaded the cord through the holder, swung the mechanism away from the boat, and lowered the hydrophone into the water. Gurgles and rippling static came through the monitor as the mike plunged into the water.

She leaned out from the rail, checking the depth of the mike. Her cutoffs rode up the back of her thighs, exposing a long, slim length of leg and a sliver of skin at her waist. She'd dressed in clothes that would have been unprovocative on any other woman. On Maria the workingman's outfit was sexier than anything he could, at the moment, imagine. She didn't wear anything black and lacy underneath it, he decided with sudden conviction. What was underneath was smooth, soft skin, and he could picture her with her hair loose over her shoulders and the kind of look in her eyes that could drive a man over the edge of control to sensual insanity. He clenched his jaw against the surge of raw desire that coursed through him.

She caught the taut expression on his face when she straightened and turned toward him. Fortunately she misinterpreted it. "All right," she said, her tone wry, "so we probably won't hear any whale songs this afternoon. It's a good lead-in for giving the customers some information about whales. And they seem to like the audible dimension."

He shrugged, directed his gaze to his can of soda, and popped the top. "Is that what got you hooked on whales? The audible dimension?"

She smiled. "Yes. In Bermuda. I was half hooked already, but one of my professors and her husband invited me to spend a few days on their boat at the winter breeding grounds. They'd been recording the humpback songs there for several years. And when I heard them . . . I was hooked for life. It was hard to describe. The water was alive with sounds sometimes. The whole ocean vibrating with strange music. It was awesome. Beautiful."

He took a sip of the soda, watching the play of emotion over her face. "When you go back there," he said, "maybe you'll recognize some of the singers."

"When I go back there?" She smiled and shook her head, but he didn't miss the glint of excitement in her eyes. "At any rate, I probably wouldn't recognize single whales. Their songs aren't individually distinctive. All the humpbacks in the Bermuda waters sing the same song."

"You can sing along, then."

She shook her head. "Not even that. The song changes every year. It evolves from one year to the next, picks up new phrases, combines old ones. And what's so strange and fascinating is that all the humpbacks are always singing the same song. As it changes, they tell each other somehow—or they change it as a group. But they're always attuned to each other, always singing the same phrases. It's"— she shrugged—"it's uncanny. Something other than human intelligence. It's a different kind of mind. They're creatures from another world."

She was watching the smooth water ahead of them, her gaze distant, her face soft, the smooth skin touched with the color of her emotion.

At his silence she glanced at him, then gave a musical laugh. "I do realize I'm probably not going to hear any whale songs off the coast of Massachusetts. But I go for the chance whenever I get out here. And most of the customers like it."

Jake nodded. "So they'll expect me to put out the hydrophone when I'm captain, huh?"

"That's right. And who knows? Maybe you'll hear something."

"Maybe I will."

She gazed at him, then gave him that slow, mesmerizing smile. "If you do, it will change your life."

Jake felt something tighten in his chest, strange and inexplicable in normal terms. Something he hadn't felt for a long, long time. Since before he'd lost his illusions in a half-million-dollar divorce deal and a humiliation that had cost, in its own way, even more.

With practiced skill he shrugged off the memory. Thinking about his past mistakes was fruitless and unpleasant. He'd done enough of it to know that. "How long do you plan to wait here?" he asked.

Her smile faded at the abrupt tone of his voice. "I don't know. That depends on what happens. And at any rate, the *Dolphin*'s got the sighting area covered. We'll know everything going on there. The radio's on. We'll hear Miguel if he identifies his whale."

Jake nodded, turning toward the rail and leaning his elbows on it. "Did you give him our coordinates?"

"Yes. Why?"

"Accidents happen," he said succinctly.

Disbelief crossed her face, and Jake felt a surge of self-disgust at his own unprofessional indiscretion. He'd said more than he intended to because he'd let his emotions get in the way of his business sense.

She started to answer him, and he braced himself for an astute question about what he suspected, but she cut off the words and instead gave him a short nod. He waited for her to change her mind and ask him, but at her continued silence he felt his apprehension about the slip change to annoyance that she hadn't, apparently, caught it.

Was she really so complacent about the accidents that she didn't recognize the possibility of sabotage? She didn't know about it having happened before, that was true, and she didn't realize the extent of Wyatt's antagonisms, but still . . . she could be in danger herself.

The thought brought with it a wave of anger he knew was out of proportion, but logic didn't seem to have much to do with it.

She could be in danger.

"You ever switch the captains on the boats?" he asked as casually as he could.

"Sometimes. If one of the captains can't come in, I'll take over. Or I'll call one of the others."

He digested the information, trying to dismiss the stab of anxiety he felt at the idea that Maria might be running one of the boats when a saboteur's work put it in danger. And she hadn't even bothered to secure the *Spiritos.*

She was frowning at his extended silence, puzzled, but when his attention stayed fixed on his soda, she turned back to the water and raised her binoculars.

Leave it at that, he told himself. Maria Santos was an experienced, competent navigator, probably in no danger she couldn't handle. If the Marlow fleet actually was subject to malicious tampering, the *Spiritos* would be low on the list of targets.

He glanced at her, taking in the classic line of her profile, her slim hand competently holding the binoculars, the nails clipped short and bare of polish. Beneath the heavy flannel shirt he could just see the shape of her breasts. She was frowning slightly, gazing into the distance, looking for whales.

And he was leaning on the rail of her boat, eating her sandwich and withholding information, thereby possibly putting her life in danger. He couldn't leave it at that.

"Does anybody else take the *Spiritos* out?"

She shook her head. "Not until now." She lowered the binoculars and looked at him. "I more or less live on board. I have a room in your grandfather's house, but anyone who wants me looks for me on the boat." The corners of her mouth tipped up. "The other day when Tome Pereira had a message for Miguel, he left it on the *Spiritos.*"

"Miguel. You always take his messages?"

She nodded. "He'd do the same for me."

Something sour churned in his stomach. "Cozy little group, aren't you?"

Her expression sobered. "They're all friends, if that's what you mean. All of the captains—and a lot of the fleet's employees—are people I've known for years."

He didn't answer.

Maria let out a breath, fingering the nylon strap of her binoculars.

"One thing you should do," he said gruffly. "Put the *Spiritos* on the security system. If I'm going to be her captain, even for a limited time, she should be insured along with the rest of the fleet. You'll save yourself a little money that way too."

She studied him a moment. "I'll have to clear it with Wyatt."

"You can probably convince him it was his idea in the first place," he said dryly. "As a matter of fact I'm surprised it wasn't. Whatever else he is, he's not usually careless with lives and property."

Her eyebrows rose into skeptical arches. "*Lives* and property?"

"That's the way the policy reads," he said short-ly.

"I see. I guess I don't actually read it on a regular basis."

He glanced at her. "I'll arrange the insurance as soon as you can get the security people here. There won't be any holdups on the agency's end."

"Anything else . . . Captain?"

He unwrapped his sandwich, took a bite of it, and turned toward the railing. "Yeah," he muttered. "You might tell Miguel he has to get his messages else-where. Like the captain's deck of his own boat."

Maria was silent while she sorted out Jake's odd, uncharacteristically arrogant attitudes and short-tempered directives. "If you're looking for negligence," she said finally, "Miguel's not your man."

"No?" He swallowed a mouthful of soda, then glanced toward her. "Whose man is he?" he asked too casually.

She blinked, then raised her eyebrows as she recognized a masculine need to establish the bounds of an age-old rivalry. "Miguel is my cousin," she said. "I've known him all my life. He's family."

He let out a long breath, and she caught a glimpse of something like elemental satisfaction in his eyes. He wouldn't acknowledge the emotion, though, and his voice remained calmly disinterested. "And what does that mean? You trust him implicitly because he's family?"

"I trust him because I've known him all my life." She waited a moment, then added, "And because he's family. Like your grandfather is to you."

A huff of cynical humor was his answer. "I'm afraid I don't know what you're talking about, Sea Sprite."

She let it pass, scanning the water again, wondering with private humor if he really knew what *he* was talking about. At any rate the subject was probably safest unmentioned. There was entirely too much chemistry between them to risk mentioning Jake's flash of misplaced jealousy.

She finished her sandwich unhurriedly, then leaned her elbows against the railing. She could sense Jake's gaze on the side of her face from time to time, suggestive, possibly, of unanswered questions, but she kept her own eyes trained on the water, content to be silent. Beside them, meaningless gurgles and water sounds came from the hydrophone's monitor.

Whale watching, as Jake undoubtedly knew, was a matter of patience, perception . . . and instinct. Maria tuned in to that indefinable instinct now, listening to the currents of the water, taking in the subtle signals of wind, tide, and temperature. She raised her binoculars again, scanned the horizon, then made a little sound in the back of her throat as a sudden, small shifting of light on the water caught her attention.

"What?" Jake asked sharply.

Her breath whooshed out. "It's gone. But I think it was a whale."

"A whale?" He raised his own glasses. "Are you sure?"

She shook her head, though he couldn't see her, his own eyes trained on the spot she'd been looking at. "I don't know," she said softly. "I think so, though."

He lowered his binoculars. "I'll start the boat," he said, pushing away from the rail. "We can get closer."

"Start the engine, run it for five seconds, then turn it off," she ordered. "If it's Joaquim, he'll find us."

Jake hesitated, half turned toward the wheelhouse. "You're kidding, right? Your whale's going to find us by the sound of your engine?"

His look was bemused, skeptical, and wary, and she laughed slightly as she looked at him. "Just do it."

"Aye, aye, Boss." He strode toward the wheelhouse to follow her instructions. The engine thrummed to life, rumbled for a few seconds, then coughed as Jake throttled it down.

"Okay, Sea Sprite," he said when he emerged from the doorway onto the deck again. "Will he come straight toward us?"

"Probably." She slanted him a quick, excited glance. "Watch. He'll surface again."

"Where?"

She pointed. He moved closer to her, marking the spot before he raised his binoculars—the skeptic doubting there would be anything to see. Smug anticipation of being right made her smile.

He glanced at her, frowning. "How the hell do you know where a whale is going to surface, when you're not even sure that's what you saw?"

Her chuckle was indulgent and very pleased. "I *don't* know. Just watch."

"Then why do I feel like I'm about to be hoodwinked by some sort of scam? What'd you do—hire a whale for the part?"

"Don't be ridiculous," she told him, deadpan. "Whales aren't for hire. It's a squadron of divers in a whale suit."

"Yeah, well I'd like to see—" His sentence stopped in his throat. In the fields of their binoculars, a mile away, a humpback whale arched from the water in a smooth, powerful leap that brought his body fifteen feet into the air. When he crashed back into the water, spray rose around him in white, sparkling sheets. A second later the sound of the distant splash reached them.

"I don't believe it," Jake muttered. "Was that your whale?"

"Looked like him."

"I'll be—" He grinned at her. "That's amazing."

She grinned back, delighted with his admiration. "It's not, really. Just a matter of experience and a little—"

"The hell it's not," he said. "It's nothing short of amazing, Sea Sprite. No one else the whole length of this coast could have predicted that."

Laughter bubbled up from her chest. "Ah . . . the skeptic converted. That's sweet revenge, Captain Marlow. I should have made you bet ten dollars on it."

"You need money as well as revenge?" he grumbled, but he chuckled with her, clearly as delighted as she. "What kind of a mercenary attitude is that?"

"Necessary," she said. "I've got pirates trying to run up the skull and crossbones on my boat. I've got to get the best of them somehow."

Mischief silvered his blue eyes. "I think you've got the best of this one all right."

"I've saved my boat, then."

"Oh, I never really wanted the boat anyway." The corners of his mouth drifted down into seriousness, and his gaze, resting on her face, darkened. "Just the owner." He was standing so close that his shoulder brushed hers, and she could see a tiny pulse beating at his temple, where the bright sunlight slanted across his face, but she made no move to back away from him. Instead she searched his face the way he was searching hers, captivated by some elemental honesty in his eyes. "You are . . . amazing, Sea Sprite."

"Oh, I don't know. 'Amazing' is in the eye of the beholder."

"Is it?"

She nodded, smiling. "Don't tell me you're looking through the wrong end of the spyglass again, Jake Marlow."

The hydrophone sighed and murmured its underwater sounds. Watching Jake and remembering how the strange sounds had affected her when she first heard them, imagining how they must affect Jake, the sensual, otherworldly cadences moved her as they wouldn't have if she'd been alone.

He reached out to touch the side of her face, ran his fingers down her cheek, then curled his palm around her neck inside the collar of her flannel shirt. His hand was warm, calloused, rough-skinned, but his touch was so gentle, she had to stop herself from leaning into it.

She went still, the last remnants of her smile fading.

"Don't tell me again you don't want me to kiss you, Maria Santos."

She should. It was exactly what she should tell him, but she said nothing . . . nothing . . . as he leaned closer. His thumb caressed the underside of her jaw, urging her chin up to position their mouths together. Her unspoken protest evaporated in the air between them just before their lips touched.

His lips were soft, warm, and ginger-ale-sweet, and as he slanted his head to fit their mouths more perfectly, her eyes fluttered closed, and her resistance melted in the lingering warmth of his kiss. Her fingers touched the back of his neck in a first tentative return of his embrace, then her hand slid into the thick, straight, unruly hair that brushed his collar.

He was holding her arm at the elbow, and she could feel the trembling of his fingers. He cupped his palm around the soft flannel of her shirt and pulled her closer, heedless of the binoculars caught between them. The uneasy warnings she'd given herself about involvement with Wyatt's grandson dissolved into the bright spring afternoon and the quickening shiver of sensuality that danced along her skin everywhere she touched him—lips, breasts, stomach, thighs.

He opened her mouth with his, using pressure and shape to communicate without words what he wanted of her. When he sought the inside of her mouth with his tongue, she met him with hers, inviting and returning the shock of deeper intimacy as her hesitation gave way to sweet, willing, undisguised need. His crossed hands cupped her lower back and pulled her hard against him.

His arousal was obvious, a blatant and unarguable communication of his body's desires. Maria felt the answer in her own body, in the shift of chemistry and biorhythm, her heart beating an erratic, sensual pattern as ancient and compelling as the sea itself.

Jake's tongue twined with hers, meeting, caressing, sliding along the sensitive inner surface of her lips, coaxing a sweet, liquid response in her body that melted every shred of resistance she'd felt. Her breath sighed out and she moved closer, ignoring the glass and metal object pressed between them as the kiss grew immediate, demanding, all-encompassing.

A second later, with no more warning than a sudden roar from the hydrophone, the ocean beside the *Spiritos* exploded in a rush of white spray. Maria gave a startled cry. The deck shifted beneath their feet on a pressure wave as twenty tons of humpback whale rose out of the water. The enormous body, half above the surface, poised for a few breathless seconds as one giant eye surveyed them from ten feet away.

Jake muttered an awestruck word his grandfather wouldn't have used in her presence as Maria leaned over the railing, stretching out her arm toward the whale. The mammoth humpback slid back into the water, churned a rolling wave with his tail, and dove under the boat.

There was a rush of sound through the hydrophone, but the whale adroitly avoided hitting it. He breached once on the other side of the boat, smashed back into the water, and with a flip of his immense tail, set his course east.

Maria was already moving toward the rod that held the hydrophone. "I'll get this," she said over her shoulder. "Start the engines. We'll follow him."

Jake hesitated, watching as the whale breached once more, as if beckoning them to give chase, then turned back to Maria. For the span of a few heartbeats they shared a strange, entranced look, caught in the disturbing sensation of having witnessed something that didn't seem real, as if the whale had been conjured up by the heat that had flared between them. Maria felt an upwelling of desire strong enough to eclipse the reality of where they were and what they were doing there, then she found her voice and forced it to say the proper words. "Go *on!*" she urged.

His mouth quirked at the corners, but the expression couldn't rightly be called a grin. "Aye, aye, Cap'n," he muttered as he turned back toward the wheelhouse.

She fought the quick, confusing urge to stop him, to call him back, to step back into his arms and forget Joaquim, the *Spiritos*, the job she was there to do, but Jake walked through the doorway into the wheelhouse, and common sense inched its way into her consciousness. Joaquim had saved her—for the moment—from temptation.

A reluctant smile curved her mouth. Maybe Jake Marlow's jealousy of a whale hadn't been so far off the mark after all.

Five

Like Moby Dick, his infamous ancestor, Joaquim led them on an open-throttle chase Jake could have sworn was intentionally mischievous. He was swimming at twenty knots, breaching every few minutes, as if to signal them. Jake held the *Spiritos* on the whale's course, but most of his attention was on the woman beside him in the wheelhouse as she watched the water through binoculars. Her eyes were glued to the spot in front of them where Joaquim would surface next. She hadn't so much as glanced at Jake since she'd come into the wheelhouse. That fact should have told him something, he decided.

Hell, it did tell him something, but his testosterone wasn't listening. She smelled of salt and warmth and something flowery and intoxicatingly feminine. His gaze slid toward her again. Her lips were slightly parted, her face flushed. The faint mark of his thumb, where he'd pressed against her cheek, was still visible. Her breathing was more rapid than normal, and there was a certain tension in her body he could feel in his own: the frantic rush of getting under way, and the elemental emotion as old as mariners and the ocean and the primitive thrill of the chase.

"Where's he taking us?" Jake shouted over the thrumming of the engines.

She lowered the binoculars and glanced at him. "There's an island ahead of us. Joaquim likes it."

"Seal's Island? The wildlife sanctuary?"

"That's right."

"That's not a whale sanctuary. What's he like about it?"

Her laugh sparkled like sun on water, and Jake felt his pulse jump in response. "Who knows? But I'll bet you anything that's where he's headed."

"Anything?"

She scanned the horizon, then grinned back at him. "There it is, Captain. I win again."

The island, actually a twin outcropping of rock, sand, and struggling vegetation bisected by a narrow channel, was dead ahead. Jake slowed the *Spiritos* as they drew toward it, glancing at Maria for an indication of which way to go around. The whale had dived in front of them moments ago. Jake scanned the water, looking for signs of him.

"There's a natural anchorage around the other side," Maria said. "Cut through the channel. It's plenty deep."

"You sure?"

"Of course."

He approached cautiously, skirting sharp, rocky cliffs on the near side of the channel, then maneuvering the *Spiritos* into the narrow passage. Why, he wondered, had Maria chosen a course that seemed to cut off their view of Joaquim's next probable appearance? At the end of the hundred-foot channel a protective rocky overhang formed a small, hidden cove. The harbor was ideal anchorage, but, enclosed by sheer cliffs, it offered little field of view.

"Here?"

She nodded.

He backed the throttle to stop their headway, then cut the engine as Maria stepped out on deck to unwind the anchor line. *Spiritos* drifted to a stop.

In the sudden quiet, Jake followed her onto the deck, glancing around him, peering southward toward the open water. Joaquim seemed to have disappeared from the ocean. "What now, Boss?"

"He'll probably come through the channel, where we did, then surface over there." She leaned on the railing and pointed with her chin.

Jake frowned back toward the channel, a passage only fifty feet wide at its narrows. "No way. He'll go around."

"Trust me, Captain."

"Trust you," Jake muttered.

She studied him for a moment, brows drawn together, then smiled. "You're still not convinced, Skeptic? All right, then." She was unbuttoning her flannel shirt as she spoke.

Jake's gaze slipped down to her fingers at the placket of her shirt. He watched, mesmerized, as she undid the buttons, revealing a white T-shirt beneath the heavy flannel. "What are you doing?"

"There's a little beach on the other side with a view of the channel."

She shrugged off her outer shirt. The white knit T-shirt pulled taut against her breasts for an instant. Jake shifted his gaze. "How are we going to get there?" he asked.

She bent down, pulling her waterproof duffel toward her and unzipping it. His sweater, lying in a corner by the wheelhouse, went into the bag along with her shirt. She untied her sneakers and stood up.

"Are you kidding?" he said, incredulous. "It's May. That water's like ice."

She toed off one sneaker. "Abandon ship, Captain. That's an order." Still grinning at him, she swung one leg over the railing, reached down for the duffel, and dropped into the water.

With a moment's disbelieving hesitation and a muttered curse, Jake took off his shoes and followed her overboard.

The shock of the cold water knocked the breath out of his lungs. "Sweet Jehosophat," he gasped. "You *are* crazy. And so am I."

"I'll race you!"

"Damn right you will!"

A scant six feet of sandy beach sloped down between the rocks of the lee island. Jake's numb feet found bottom just before hers did, and he waded to shore, snatching up the duffel with one arm and reaching for Maria with the other. She put her hand in his and followed him through the cold surf and up the gentle slope of the sun-warmed beach. Grinning at him, she dropped to the sand, leaning back on her hands.

Jake flopped onto the beach next to her, hands folded behind his head, and scowled.

She chuckled. "What's the matter, Captain? Is the challenge of whale watching too much for you?"

"Whale watching?" He gaped at her comically. "I was seduced overboard, damn near drowned, flash frozen, and some of my most treasured anatomical parts are shriveled to the size of raisins. You call this whale watching?"

"I didn't seduce you overboard."

"Of course you did," he grumbled. "Why else would I have jumped in?"

She braced herself on one arm, facing him, and he turned his head to watch her. "You were chasing a whale," she said smugly.

Her T-shirt, plastered to her body, revealed the shape of her breasts, the nipples puckered beneath the cold, wet material. Wet cutoffs outlined the curve of her hip, the line of her thigh. His gaze slipped down over her seated figure, then traveled back up again. "A whale. Yeah."

She straightened self-consciously and leaned forward for the duffel. "Do you want your sweater?"

"No." He shook his head. "That water is so cold, I feel warm just getting out of it."

She laughed, fumbling with stiff fingers at the zipper. The clinging T-shirt outlined the slim, strong curve of her back, from the vulnerable curve of her neck to the hollow where her jeans pulled away from her waist. A sprinkle of goose bumps raised the fine hairs along her bare arm and the smooth length of thigh below her shorts. Jake swallowed, feeling heat course into his body.

"Look," she said softly, staring along the channel that separated the two islands. Her hands were still on the zipper.

Jake sat up. He could see nothing definable, but across the surface of the water there was something. . . .

His throat tightened on a sense of expectation he couldn't quantify.

Suddenly the water at the opening of the passage boiled with the heavy, rolling lift of a twenty-foot flipper, and through the passage in front of them an immense body, plowing up a split wave, churned just below the surface, moving so fast, Jake involuntarily flinched away from the water.

Maria had turned to watch the whale. "He's going to breach," she murmured. She touched his arm. "Watch him."

Just beyond the island the immense humpback rose out of the water, his huge body defying all the laws of gravity for a moment before he crashed back into the ocean in an explosion of spray. Maria's laughing gasp as her hand tightened on his arm was the only sound either of them made. Behind the whale, the wave of his reentry rushed along the rocky cliffs and washed over the beach at their feet, an aftershock of energy that echoed the force of an immense and powerful creature who'd demonstrated—for reasons no logic could tell—his mastery of the sea.

Jake had never witnessed anything remotely like it. Not in his experience, not in his imagination. Maria was right, he realized. There was no way to understand it by logic. It had to be sensed in the bones, by instinct. By intuition, passion . . . the kind of passion Maria felt for these creatures she stalked. The kind of passion no logic in the world could withstand.

He felt it now, welling up, charging through a narrow channel, surging out of the sea as if it would defy any dictates placed on it.

Maria's hand was still touching his arm. She was shivering, from cold and from reaction, her breathing faster than normal, her breasts inside the clinging T-shirt rising and falling with each breath.

"Maria," he said. The word was a hoarse command.

Her eyes flicked toward him, wide and questioning.

He swept his arm around her shoulders, turning

her to him, and bent his head to hers. She gave a small, startled sound of surprise as he pulled her closer, then her hand tightened on his arm as he lowered her to the sand, cradling her head against his forearm. His lips touched her mouth and took it, twisting urgently to seal the kiss, opening her lips to the thrusting, possessive penetration of his tongue. Her mouth was sweet, intimate, warm as hot honey in contrast to her cold nose against his cheek, her cold, wet shoulders under his hands.

A wave of desire, potent as the wake of the whale that had just passed their private beach, coursed through him. He went under it, as surely as if he'd been washed overboard in a savage North Atlantic storm. Discipline, restraint, caution—all the qualities that had governed his life since he'd left the fleet disappeared in a flood of desire too strong to resist as she surrendered to the kiss, pliant, sweet, and willing beneath him. She shivered once, and he cupped her shoulder, warming her cold skin through the T-shirt, sheltering her small, fragile body with his own, willing her the heat of his passion.

She made a sound in the back of her throat, a moan of satisfaction or need, and he plundered her mouth once more in an act of prerogative stronger than reason. He wanted her. Her lithe, strong body, her quick intelligence, the passion she gave to her whales. He wanted her acknowledgment that she was his; that she'd been meant for him before they met; that she would belong to him in an uncharted future. It made no sense. But sense had nothing to do with this visceral, primitive surge of possessiveness.

His lips blazed a hot, damp trail down her neck to the hollow of her throat, and he slid his leg over hers. The friction of wet denim over skin pulled his jeans taut against his hard arousal. He sucked in his stomach and rolled to one hip, taking her with him, following some ancient instinct of courtship that warned not to threaten her with passion she was not yet ready to return in full measure.

"Sea Sprite," he murmured against her throat, "what you do to me is unreal."

She let out a sighing breath and threaded her hand into his hair, along his shoulders, across his back. She was strong, feminine, intoxicatingly sensual as she arched her back and pulled his head down to the gap where the neck of her T-shirt vee'd at her collarbone.

The unexpectedly sweet immediacy of her response stirred emotions that blurred the border between passion and protectiveness, pleasure given and pleasure taken. He was supporting her with an arm around her shoulders, his hand on her back, where already he could feel the faint heat of warm skin beneath the wet cloth.

He traced the neckline of her shirt with his lips, then moved his head lower to nuzzle at the valley between her breasts, where her shirt was gathered in folds. His mouth followed the swell of her breast to its peak, then he opened his lips over cold cloth and warm flesh and the hard, pebbled bud of her nipple, gathered in the heat of his mouth into a tight knot of desire. His tongue shaped and caressed her through the wet, salty cloth until she writhed beneath him, arching her back to strain toward his mouth.

Her moan filled him with a fierce, surging satisfaction. *Yes, Sea Sprite. Burn for me. Let me make you burn.* He wasn't sure whether he'd said the words aloud. He only knew he wanted her passion. He wanted her release as much as he wanted his own. More. Somewhere in the ocean that stretched around them a creature of power and immensity had made her breathless with awe, and Jake needed to work his own effect on her, leave his own stamp.

His mouth still at her breast, he slid his hand down to her shorts, tracing the heavy denim down to the hem, then inching his fingers up her thigh. Her skin was silken smooth, damp, cool. When he cupped her buttocks, encased in silky wet nylon, she arched against him and shifted her hips. His free hand found her other breast and he stroked the sweetly rigid nipple, shaped and reshaped her soft flesh. She tasted of salt and felt like velvet, and the sweet sigh that came from her mouth stoked a primitive surge of desire that nearly drove him over the edge. He wanted to strip off her shorts and her panties and claim her from the inside out, surround himself with her lush warmth and sweet compliance and intoxicating passion and drive himself into her, again and again, until they both exploded with mindless, insensate ecstasy.

The violent urgency of his need shook him. He lifted his head to study her face, his hand circling her neck, his thumb caressing her swollen lower lip. "Maria."

Her eyes fluttered open and met his, dark and luminous with an inner fire.

"Maria . . ." He hesitated over the words, thinking of the little foil packages in his duffel on board the *Spiritos*.

The question needed asking.

Her brows drew together, and her passion-darkened gaze focused on his face. Jake's words trailed off before they started. He knew with growing certainty he didn't need to ask any questions. She hadn't planned this. She wasn't prepared.

He dropped back flat on the warm sand, taking

her with him, cradling the slight weight of her body on his. He shut his eyes, squeezing her buttock with careful, protracted pressure, gathering his control. "It's all right, Sea Sprite," he murmured. "I know you're not protected. I won't make you pregnant."

She blinked, comprehension coming into her face. A wash of color flared in her cheeks. Her face was shadowed, the sun behind her head forming a nimbus around her wet hair. Jake cupped the back of her head, instinctively holding her as he watched her pull herself back from the edge of desire.

"No," she said, her voice shaky. "No, I wouldn't have let it go that far."

He didn't like the phrasing of that. Or the way she'd gone utterly still, her gaze on his face. Some fierce protest clenched in his gut.

His hand slid up her leg, between their bodies, until he found the warmth at the junction of her thighs. He pressed with the heel of his hand, caressing through wet denim, as if he would ignore all physical barriers between them the way he wanted to ignore the more subtle barriers.

She held herself still, though he could sense her effort to deny her own response. The muscles of her stomach tightened, and regret flickered across her face. "Jake, I . . ."

He stopped her with one hand against her lips. "Don't say that, Sea Sprite. Don't think it." But she was thinking it. He could feel her pulling away from him, moving back from the intimacy they'd come so close to. *No.* The word was lodged behind his clenched jaw, the unreleased tension in his body almost unbearable. He brushed his hand down her back, along her rib cage, over her hip. "Stay with me, Maria. I need you."

Her breath was a shuddering, warm sigh of desire, but she inched away from him, untangling her legs from his and settling on the sand beside him, knees hugged to her chest.

Jake gritted his teeth to keep himself from grasping her legs and hauling her back over him where he wanted her. Instead he let her go, closing his eyes again and pulling in deep gulps of air, willing his body to back down, to let her go.

"I'm sorry, Jake," she said softly. "I shouldn't have let this happen. I shouldn't have brought you over here. I could have predicted . . ."

He turned his head toward her.

The corners of her lips twitched in a wry sketch of a smile. "I should have known this would happen when I lured you into that water. We should have stayed on the boat."

"If we'd stayed on the boat," he said, the words a gruff moan, "we'd be within reach of my duffel bag, and we wouldn't have a problem."

Her expression became serious. "It's not a birth-control problem, Jake. Going back to the *Spiritos* won't solve it. I can't make love to you."

He raised himself on one elbow, then slowly and deliberately reached for her. His fingers grazed her cheek, then he traced the line of her jaw with his knuckles. When he brushed his thumb over her lower lip, it trembled.

"You could, Maria," he murmured, his voice husky. "When I touch you, you melt like ice on hot sand. I can't believe you do that every time someone touches you. Every time someone wants to."

"I don't—"

His hand closed around her shoulder, hard, as if to force her to his will. "Dammit, you can't deny that."

She drew in a long breath. "I'm not denying it."

At her softly voiced admission he loosened his hold on her shoulder, caressing instead of compelling, both his hand and his breathing unsteady. He didn't want to dominate her. What he wanted was something far more complex, far less easily claimed.

"There's something that happens," she said. "But it's . . . not enough, Jake."

"How could it not be enough when you don't know what it is?" He slid his hand up to her neck, caressing her throat. "Let me show you."

Her own hand closed over his, stopping him. "I don't think I need another demonstration, Jake," she said, smiling slightly.

A momentary flare of anger overrode his ache of frustrated longing, and he let his hand drop away from her. Slowly he pushed himself up on the sand, leaning on one straight arm. "What's between us doesn't deserve a snide remark, Maria. Say no if you have to, but not like that."

She blinked, startled. "I'm sorry. But . . . I've said it every other way I can think of."

His gaze dropped to her mouth. "Except the way that really means it."

She turned away from him, toward the water. When she looked back, something vulnerable in her face made him shut his eyes for a moment, denying what he didn't want to see. He hadn't meant to say something so hard-edged, after he'd chided her for the same thing.

"Did you ever come to this beach before?" she asked him.

"No."

She scooped up a handful of sand, letting it slip out through her fingers. "Places like this . . ." She glanced at him. "I was a town girl in a summer resort. Places like this were where you came to have a one-night fling."

"Did you have any?" he asked tightly.

He thought she wasn't going to answer, but she said finally, "One. It was enough to let me know I couldn't handle it." She met his eyes and shrugged. "Still can't."

"So you're going to shut me off because you had your heart broken when you were sixteen? You're not a town girl anymore, Maria. You're a grown woman. And I'm not a tourist."

Her T-shirt was still plastered to her body. She made no attempt to rearrange it, but pulled her knees up to her chest and wrapped her arms around them, making herself less vulnerable, less accessible. "No," she said. "You're not going to be here long enough to be a tourist. You'll be gone in a few weeks, maybe less. The fact is you're only here because you had to make sure I'm capable of managing your grand-father's fleet."

"Maria—"

"No," she cut him off. "You have a right to your concern about the business. You have a right to know whether I'm capable. But anything else wasn't meant to be. There just isn't enough . . . trust between us. There wasn't from the start." Her voice dropped. "I'm sorry."

"Trust." She glanced up sharply at his cynical tone. A stab of dismay thinned his mouth, and he shook his head as if to dismiss it. "My grandfather hired you," he said. "He wouldn't have done it if he hadn't thought you were capable."

"So why didn't you trust his judgment?"

"That's not the point, dammit! I wanted to make

sure he really had stepped down, that he wasn't still trying to run the business."

"Because you were concerned for his health?" Her tone held a note of skepticism.

"Yes," Jake said shortly. "That's part of it."

Her eyes searched his face, steady and faintly antagonistic, puzzling out what part he hadn't told her. "Of course he's still involved in it. He's still worrying about it. Did you expect him to turn that part over to you?"

"I'm not trying to take over his business. And no one else is going to either."

"No one else?" Her voice rose in surprise. Clearly it wasn't what she'd expected to hear. "Who are you talking about? Me?"

Jake said nothing, calculating the effect of an answer.

He didn't need to give it. He could see comprehension spread over her face. "You're talking about the accidents," she said incredulously. "You think someone's causing these accidents because they want to take over the fleet. That's what you're investigating."

Again he said nothing.

"Isn't it?" she snapped.

"Yes."

She didn't move.

He'd wanted her to guess. Maybe he'd set it up so that she would. "It's happened before," he said flatly. "Eight years ago somebody was sabotaging the fleet. The criminal was never caught, because he stopped when he realized someone was on to him. Wyatt didn't bother to tell you about that. I know he didn't."

She drew in a sharp breath, then shook her head.

"My grandfather's made a lot of enemies over the years," Jake went on. "There are plenty who have reason to be glad he's not as strong as he once was. If someone's trying to get back at him—or take over the fleet—they'd be crazy to pass up this chance."

"You're talking about . . . sabotage," she said.

He nodded.

"And you're trying to find out who might have moved in to take advantage of your grandfather."

He didn't like the shocked, quiet tone of her voice. "Look—maybe there's no one doing anything. Maybe it's all just a series of accidents. Bad luck. But I'm not just going to trust to that."

"Of course not. You don't trust luck. Or instinct. Or . . . who your grandfather hires as a manager." She stood up, moving calmly and deliberately, as if she had to be careful of how she moved, and walked toward the water.

Jake let her take one step, telling himself not to react, before he went after her and snatched at her arm. "Dammit, Maria, you can't trust people when you're investigating a possible sabotage. What do you want from me? I can't go to the police with this. Wyatt would have another heart attack. I can't even mention it to *him*."

"Or to me either," she said. "Did you think I was sabotaging your grandfather's fleet?"

He hesitated a moment too long.

She muttered something in Portuguese and turned away from him.

"Maria—" When he pulled her around to face him again, he saw a bright gleam of moisture in her eyes.

He let her go, appalled at the evidence that he had hurt her, feeling the weight of guilt settle around him as his anger dissipated.

She reached down to pick up the duffel, keeping her

back to him, careful not to accuse him of anything. The simple dignity of the gesture pulled at some emotion deep in his gut. He didn't have a name for it, but it ached as if some part of him was being torn away.

He took a couple of steps toward her and held his hand out for the duffel. "I'll go back to the *Spiritos* and get one of the lifeboats," he said. "I'll come back for you."

She stared at him for a moment, her eyes still too bright. "No," she said softly. "I'm a town girl, Jake. I can swim."

He watched her wade up to her thighs into the cold water, then dive under it. He flinched at the cold splash, feeling that tug of emotion in his gut again.

She could swim. He knew that. She didn't need to be rowed back to her boat in a gesture that was meant as a half-assed apology. Dammit, he'd wanted to tell her the first time he'd met her. But it hadn't been a choice. He was caught between his grandfather and a multimillion-dollar fleet, with barely enough options to keep both the fleet and the grandfather from going under. Trust was a luxury he couldn't afford.

And—*dammit*—it was a surefire path to getting hurt. To hurt and disillusionment . . . and tears. Didn't she *know* that by now?

He snatched up the duffel, heaved it as far out into the channel as he could, then sprinted in after it and dove.

The North Atlantic was just a little colder than any facts he had to face.

Six

Within two days, the *Spiritos* was wired to the fleet's
security system. Jake was as good as his word on that
project. About everything else he'd been completely
silent.

Maria fought back the lonely, hurt emptiness that
claimed all the places in herself he'd filled with laughter. They had nothing to say to each other, she told
herself. He owed her no explanation for conducting an
undercover investigation, and she didn't want one.

And anyway what she felt for Jake Marlow wasn't
going to be changed by reasonable explanations.

She wanted—needed—days out on the water with
the *Spiritos,* but knowing Jake's real purpose there
meant she had to concede him the use of her boat
until he found whatever answers he was looking
for and left the boat and the sea to get on with
his life. He was there as an insurance investigator,
she reminded herself whenever she thought of him.
He hadn't gotten to know her for personal reasons.
He had a job to do. And so did she.

But constant, sensual images of Jake haunted her
long, aimless walks on the beach and distracted her
concentration even at work.

When she walked into Wyatt's study at the house

late one afternoon to give him the day's report, she found him with Jake's old spyglass balanced across one knee. She stopped where she was, hand on the door. Her casual greeting stalled in her throat, replaced by a sudden ache of longing and a picture so vivid, she thought it must be visible to her employer.

"Well, come in," Wyatt muttered irritably.

She stepped in and closed the door behind her, swallowing hard and summoning the sense of outrage that had carried her through the past few days. When she met Wyatt's gaze, he was frowning back at her.

"It's an old-fashioned spyglass," he barked. "You don't have to stare at it like I'm balmy. My grandson left it here."

"I know what it is," she said.

"Damned insult. He thinks I can't see to the end of the dock. Told him there's not much goes on at my dock I don't know about already."

"That's hard to argue with, Wyatt."

The older man grunted, then turned toward the window. "The *Dolphin* was late coming back."

"I know. Miguel didn't expect the offshore wind. They made poor time on the return trip."

"The caterer's truck was here waitin' for him."

The caterer's truck? She frowned. "Again?"

"Yep." Wyatt slanted her a look. "Does your cousin Miguel have some undercover deal on candy bars?"

A flicker of uneasiness stalled her answer for a moment. *Miguel?* The unwanted suspicion was rejected almost as soon as she'd formed it, but the afterimage was disturbing. What would Jake make of that information if he heard it? He was all but convinced the accidents in the fleet had been sabotage, carried out by someone who worked for Marlow Enterprises. "Miguel's well known for his sweet tooth," she said. "Maybe he's been raiding the larder."

"He's been findin' whales, anyway," Wyatt said. "They all have. Even my grandson."

He peered at her, making a querulous gesture with the spyglass. "You know what he said when he gave me this? Told me to keep an eye on your boat. Got some fool notion it's going to float away on the tide if I don't watch it. And he made darn sure it was hooked up to the security before you took it out again."

Maria glanced toward the window overlooking the Marlow dock. Her boat's new security box glowed like a tiny votive light in front of her slip.

She kept her voice even, but the ache was back in her throat. "He's running the *Spiritos*. It's only natural he'd be concerned about her. He's a good captain."

Wyatt was watching her, his expression shrewd. "That so?"

"You should know it. He used to work for you."

"He doesn't work for me now."

Maria stared at Wyatt, while the words *Yes, he does* slipped into her mind. She glanced away, resenting the charged network of facts that couldn't be acknowledged. Reporting to Wyatt was like navigating a treacherously bottomed harbor.

Wyatt's eyes narrowed on her. "My grandson lost most of that insurance company of his to his ex-wife five years after he started it. Did you know that?"

"No," she said, startled at the abrupt disclosure.

"A gold digger," Wyatt spat out. "A smart, tough one. Taught him a lesson he won't forget—how to stick to business. He made back all the money he lost, and then some. He didn't do it by chasin' whales. Whatever else he might have chased, he throws it back when he's done—always."

Maria crossed her arms in front of her, feeling a lump of unwanted longing lodged in her chest like a held breath. "None of that is any of my business, Wyatt."

"Why not? Did you send him packing?"

She swallowed hard as anger stiffened her fragile emotions. "And that's none of yours."

"Huh." Chastened, the older man turned toward the window, then tugged on one ear and glanced back at her. "Maybe not," he admitted. "But the problem is I'm not *allowed* to be mindin' my own business. Got nothin' to think about but everybody else's. What do you expect me to do, sittin' here all day?"

"I doubt you could know more of what's going on than you seem to now," she said wryly.

Wyatt huffed. "I don't know what in the name of Judas my grandson's doing here. I don't know that."

Maria's expression sobered as she contemplated her employer, feeling an ambivalent sympathy for him. She hadn't guessed what Jake was doing there herself—maybe she hadn't wanted to. But Wyatt knew about the past "accidents" to the fleet. He'd chosen not to share that information with her. Had the connection really never occurred to him? Was he being willfully blind, or just stubborn in refusing to acknowledge a danger he couldn't cope with?

"Your grandson has a substantial investment here," she said carefully.

"His investment's doing fine," Wyatt barked. "Does he think I'm going to let the business fail just because I got sick? I'm not ready to give it up yet! I hired a damn good manager, and I made sure everything else is run the same way it was when I did it myself. No new contractors, no new books, no new captains." His lip curled. "With one exception to that," he added pointedly. "And you hired him, not me."

"The *Spiritos* is my boat," she said with an edge to her voice. "I'll hire a captain if I think I need one."

"And take the consequences?"

"If there are any, yes."

"You think you're tough enough for that?"

"I'm as tough as I need to be, Wyatt."

"If you're dealing with my grandson, I doubt it."

Her temper snapped. "Then why did you hire me?"

"Because you're a damn good manager," he shot back. "And you've done a damn good job. And because I know how to appreciate hard work and loyalty, and a person who tells the straight truth the way they see it." He stared at her, his mouth quirked, then his hand tightened on the spyglass and he said gruffly, "And if that's what you've got to offer, you'd be a damn fool to offer it to someone like my grandson."

It wasn't what she'd expected. Maria felt her anger dissolve into surprise and exasperation, and a quick sheen of moisture filled her eyes. Wyatt's harsh words covered more than a concern for her own emotional vulnerability. He'd been hurt himself by what he'd interpreted as Jake's betrayal. He was speaking his own heart. She knew it, if he didn't.

She shut her eyes for a moment, feeling again that ache in her throat. It wasn't facts that were tough to face, it was emotions, feelings that threatened all of them, as surely as some outside force might threaten the fleet.

"I think," she said slowly, "at the bottom of it Jake's on your side, Wyatt."

The older man jutted his chin and scowled at her. "So you're going to trust him, then?"

The question hung between them like an unmade decision. Wyatt turned back to the window, rolling Jake's spyglass between his palms. Glancing down at his hands, he made a sound of irritation and flipped the brass toy toward an overstuffed chair in the opposite corner of the room.

Maria watched as it thudded into the padded seat and rolled to the side of the cushion.

Don't tell me you're looking through the wrong end of the spyglass, Jake Marlow.

Don't tell me you don't want me to kiss you. . . .

She had wanted it. She'd wanted more. She'd wanted loyalty and trust and straight truth, and she'd been hurt for it. But denying feelings didn't make them hurt less, any more than knowing they were foolish made them go away.

She was human, with all the complex, contradictory, unwisely given emotions of the human heart. There wasn't any shared song that wove those emotions together and bonded them into an all-encompassing harmony of spirit. She belonged to a species that fashioned glass and metal into an instrument for spying on each other. A species where trust was in shorter supply than ingenuity, and those who trusted were sometimes hurt.

But those who didn't paid a price too.

She crossed the room to the chair and picked up the spyglass. Jake was conducting an undercover investigation on possible sabotage in the fleet. Much as she didn't want to know that, she did know it, and as manager of the fleet she was obligated to cooperate. Jake needed to know anything unusual that had been observed on the dock, including the information Wyatt had given her. "I'll take this back to Jake if you don't want it here," she said.

"Might as well."

She turned to go out the door.

"I'm not blind yet," Wyatt called after her.

She only nodded, but there was an answering comment in the back of her mind. *Ele que mao quer ver.*

Wyatt wasn't blind. His observation of the *Dolphin* proved that. He had a bigger problem. He was one who would not see.

Maria climbed the front stairs and followed the hallway Mrs. Salintes kept buffed to a self-respecting shine. She knew which door was Jake's. It was the room he'd grown up in—at the back of the hallway, Jake had told her dryly, so that he couldn't sneak in and out unnoticed.

Trust, she thought, must always have been in short supply in the Marlow household.

She glanced down at the brass spyglass, then raised her hand and knocked. There was silence just long enough to make her realize she was holding her breath, then she heard footsteps crossing the room, and Jake opened the door.

He was dressed like a Saturday-morning business-man, in slightly wrinkled chinos and the white shirt he'd had on the day she met him on the dock, now worn with cuffs turned up and collar unbuttoned. His face was more deeply tanned than it had been a few days ago, and his eyes, by contrast, were a more intense blue. He stared back at her with his hand on the door and his tall, lean body poised in mid-step in the doorway. Any illusions that they had only a professional connection vanished like a receding wave on a sandy beach.

A long moment of silence told her he hadn't expected to confront her outside his door. His gaze swept over her, then returned to her face. He didn't speak.

"Hi," she said finally. When he didn't give the expected response, she found herself at a loss, standing in the doorway as awkwardly as he. A nervous chuckle finally loosened her throat. "Sorry to take you by surprise, Captain. Should I have made an appointment?"

He gazed back at her for another few seconds, then a slow, sexy smile turned up the corners of his mouth. "No, it wouldn't have made any difference. I've been picturing you for three days in a wet T-shirt. The change of clothes would have been a shock anyway."

She ordered herself not to blush, but the rampantly sensual image his confession aroused sent the blood rushing to her head.

"I'm sorry," he said with that self-deprecating charm she found irresistible.

She shrugged and dropped her gaze to her hands. She could feel his gaze follow the direction of hers, and she held the spyglass out to him. "You left this in Wyatt's study," she said. "He . . . wanted you to know he's not blind yet."

He took the spyglass from her, giving it a thoughtful shake before he closed his fist around it and lowered it to his side. "I asked him to keep an eye on the *Spiritos*."

"Yes. He mentioned that. You didn't need to ask, apparently. 'Not much goes on at my dock I don't know about,' was the way he put it."

"He didn't put it quite so diplomatically when he was talking to me."

She nodded. "No, I don't imagine he did. He can be difficult."

"Yeah."

She clasped her hands in front of her in a formal, Old World gesture, as an uncomfortable silence descended around them once more, then she met his eyes.

"You didn't tell him what I'm doing here," Jake stated.

She shook her head. "He doesn't want to believe there could be anything wrong."

"Yeah. His pride's at stake. He'd hand over the fleet on a silver platter rather than admit he has a weakness. God help anyone who implies it."

She frowned, troubled. "Yes. You're right. He can't admit he doesn't still have full control. But if there is a serious threat to the fleet, he'll have to know."

"He's not likely to listen to reason. He's convinced all the captains are completely trustworthy."

"So am I."

Jake let out a long breath into the suddenly taut silence. "And what if you're wrong? You're in for a hell of a hard landing, Sea Sprite."

"Then I'm wrong." Impulsively she touched his arm. "I'll deal with it. So will your grandfather. Don't worry so much, Jake."

He broke the contact of their eyes, looking down at her fingers on his arm. Conscious, suddenly, of the implications in her gesture, she drew her hand back, crossing her arms and tucking her fingers behind her elbows.

Jake's gaze burned its way down to her waist, where her hands were hidden in the folds of her cotton sweater, then, slowly, he raised it again to her face. He stepped back, opening the door wider. "Look, you don't have to stand here. Come in and sit down."

Behind him she saw a tall chest of drawers, a boy's single bed, floor-to-ceiling bookshelves holding what looked to be years of collected books—an intimate glimpse of a boyhood she was admittedly too curious about. "No." She shook her head. "No, thanks. I've been sitting all day, doing the accounts."

He shoved one hand into his pocket and pulled the door open even wider. "So come in and stand up. Check out the view. Let me show you my etchings."

In spite of herself she smiled, but she also shook her head. "No, I don't think so."

"Why not?"

Why not? The outrageous question brought to mind a host of outraged answers: because she was angry . . . because she couldn't forgive him for lying to her . . . because she'd written him out of her mind and hadn't thought of him in days. Not one of them was true, though. And not one of them explained the butterflies deep in her stomach and the rapid beat of her pulse.

She met his intense gaze with her own steady and honest look. "Because if I see you again, I'll end up in a wet T-shirt on another private beach."

"Is that so bad?" His voice was husky, with a catch of sincerity that did things to her insides. "Maria. I can't step on board the *Spiritos* without thinking about you. I can't talk to any of the passengers without deliberately putting you out of my mind. I see your damn whale out there and I feel like I'm being taunted because he knows you'll still be seeing him when I'm just a minor blip in your memory."

She shut her eyes against his all-too-convincing face and all-too-tempting body. "Joaquim's right," she said. "I will still be seeing him. You will be just a minor . . ." She trailed off, at a loss for the right word.

"Maria." He reached toward her, his shoulders tensed with pent-up emotions. His warm palm closed around her arm. "I'm trying to say I'm sorry. I got to know you under . . . false pretenses. I'd like to start over."

It was tempting. He tempted her with emotions that were all but irresistible, but . . . she was still caught between Jake and Wyatt, her job and her personal aspirations, her goals and the place she had started from. And she would still be there when Jake Marlow left.

She glanced down at his hand, but made no move to pull away. "I didn't come here . . . just to return the spyglass, Jake. There was something else."

He frowned.

"Your grandfather's been watching the dock. He's noticed that the caterer's been coming more often than usual. Especially to the *Dolphin.*"

"Your cousin Miguel's boat."

"Yes."

He let out a long breath and reluctantly let go of her arm. "And you think . . . ?"

"I don't think anything—least of all that Miguel would have anything to do with criminal sabotage. If there *is* criminal sabotage. But I don't want to give you any reason to think I'm withholding information. I'm . . . in a precarious position, after all. I'm one of the suspects."

He swore under his breath, viciously enough to make her eyebrows rise. It wasn't anything she'd never heard before, but Jake, like his grandfather, hadn't used it in front of her.

"You're not a suspect," he said shortly. "I know you're not sabotaging the fleet."

"Oh?" Her eyebrows rose farther. "And how do you know that? Instinct?"

He swore again, this time loudly.

Half smiling at the outburst, she started to turn away.

"Maria . . . I didn't have much choice about this. I'm sorry. I didn't want to lie to you, but I didn't have the option of exempting people from investigation. You have to understand that."

The frustrated anguish in his voice forced her to look back at him. "I do understand that," she said, meaning it. And then, more softly, "I do."

He didn't try to stop her from walking away, but she felt his gaze on her all the way down the hall.

There was no sound of a closing door.

Two hours later Jake stood at his bedroom window, staring out at the dock, watching the wind whip the harbor into foam and trying to forget the image of Maria Santos on a calm, sunny beach in a wet T-shirt and cutoffs. All the lithe, lush curves and shadowed feminine hollows of her body . . .

It wasn't going to work. He knew that. He'd been trying to forget her for three days now, without success. The scene outside his window didn't offer nearly enough distraction to erase the picture, but if he exercised enough self-discipline, his mind wouldn't go the next step to the way she'd responded to him . . . the warmth and welcome of her mouth, the way her skin had heated at his touch, the achingly sweet gathering of her nipples into hungry, rounded pebbles of desire. She'd arched toward him and made a sound in the back of her throat. . . .

Jake clenched his jaw against the groan caught in his own throat.

She doesn't want to see you. She's pointed out some damn good reasons why it's a lousy idea. And she's right. You don't have anything to offer her, Marlow. And she knows that.

He knew it too. It was what had kept him silent while he let her walk away, staring after her like a fool. She'd offered him trust, honesty, the sweet, warm passion of a woman who didn't hedge her emotional bets with an insurance policy. And she'd been hurt by that trust. He'd hurt her. Why should she let him get close enough to do it again?

But maybe if he touched her once more, she'd heat up the way she had on the beach. . . .

Jake let his breath hiss out through his teeth, cursing himself for a fool. He could use a dive into that cold water now. He'd been staring at it for the better part of two hours, and what he had for his trouble was the conviction that he was on his way to being crazier than his grandfather. In disgust at himself, he dropped the curtain and raked his hand through his hair.

He'd already decided he had to go out somewhere— anywhere—when he caught a movement on the dock. Miguel Douro strode down it, his steps jaunty, his jacket flapping in the wind. He punched in the code to the *Dolphin's* security system and hopped down onto the boarding deck.

There was nothing peculiar about his presence. The Marlow captains were encouraged to check on their boats at off-hours if they felt the urge. Jake himself had taken advantage of the practice to learn what he could from "casual" questions about the fleet's accidents, but he hadn't yet found the opportunity to talk to Douro. On this Friday night Miguel was dressed in creased trousers and sports jacket, and didn't look as if he planned a prolonged visit. If Jake wanted to talk to him, now was the time. He reached for his sweatshirt and left the room.

Outside, a stiff on-shore breeze whipped his clothes against his body and held the boats taut on their lines. A light showed in the *Dolphin*'s wheelhouse, and the door from the deck stood open.

"Miguel!" Jake called from the dock.

Miguel's head appeared in the doorway, then he waved. "What can I do for you?"

Jake stepped onto the boarding plank. "The *Spiritos* is out of coffee," he said, using the first excuse that came to mind. "Can you spare me a couple of pounds?"

"Sure," Miguel said, though Jake could hear the puzzlement in his voice.

Jake crossed the deck to the galley. He flicked on the lights as Miguel came down the stairs behind the sandwich bar.

"The food service was just here," Miguel told him as he opened the galley's storage locker. "They didn't leave coffee with *Spiritos*?"

In the locker were half a dozen bags of coffee, and beside them a stack of crates marked COFFEE CREAMER. Enough, Jake thought ironically, for a two-month supply. If the *Spiritos* was as well stocked, the chance of running out of anything was zero to nil. "I forgot to mention it," Jake said. Miguel said nothing, and Jake added, "There are a lot of things to remember in running a boat."

"True enough."

On the deck a gust of wind rattled a line. "The food service doesn't seem to have a regular schedule either," Jake commented. "I thought they were supposed to come on Thursdays."

Miguel nodded. "The driver will stop in sometimes just to see if we need anything."

"Do you need supplies that often?"

Miguel shrugged. "The man who runs the food service is ambitious, wants to increase his business. He's always looking for a chance to branch out, make more money."

It seemed a logical enough probability, and there was nothing in Miguel's informal manner to arouse suspicion. Jake took the coffee and tucked it under his arm. "Thanks," he said. "Glad I caught you before you went out."

"Maria could have let you into the galley."

Jake grinned. "And I'd have to explain how I let the *Spiritos* run out of coffee. She wouldn't be impressed."

There was a short, assessing silence. "You trying to impress her?"

The tone of voice stopped Jake for a moment, then he covered his reaction and made his own voice casual. "She's the boss."

"Yes." Miguel slammed the food locker shut and latched the door. He straightened and turned back to Jake. "Also—she's my cousin," he said. "We grew up together."

"So she told me." Miguel wasn't the only one being checked out, Jake thought wryly.

"I have a date tonight." Miguel smiled. "Lucy Pereira. My fiancée. I don't keep her waiting."

"It's never good policy to keep a woman waiting."

"I don't know about policy," Miguel said. "Just about this one woman."

Jake glanced back at him.

"One woman, one lifetime. That's all a man needs."

Jake hadn't heard the expression before, but it had the flavor of a much-repeated quotation, and the unexpected power to bring images to mind. A life spent going to sea, then coming home to a wife who made the work satisfying even when the fishing was slow, the weather harsh, the sea hostile, the tide too high, as it was that night. *One woman.*

He swallowed hard. *Right, Marlow,* he told himself sarcastically. One man, one woman. One divorce court. It was a long time since he'd had illusions about lifetime love.

Miguel was watching him, his expression assessing. "An admirable goal," Jake said, his voice more bitter than he intended.

"In my family it is more than a goal." Miguel shrugged, elaborately casual. "You've probably heard as much, from Maria."

"We haven't talked about family."

"No? She has a big family. Three brothers, five cousins."

Jake smiled crookedly. "You can tell them all I'm not seeing Maria. I'm just running her boat."

Miguel nodded. "Good night, then."

Jake picked up his coffee and let himself out of the galley.

Three brothers, five cousins. He had a vision of walking the plank into shark-infested waters while Maria's guardian relatives looked on.

On the dock he paused, feeling the first drops of rain, wind-driven and sharp and picturing Miguel watching him. He should, he supposed, take the coffee to the *Spiritos.* The light in the boat's cabin was on. Maria was on board, still up.

He let out a long breath.

Or he could bring the coffee back to the house and take it out to the boat with him tomorrow morning. There wasn't any real reason to visit Maria tonight. She'd told him herself that she didn't want to see him. His feet started to move, slowly.

Because if I see you again, I'll end up in a wet T-shirt on another private beach.

The honesty in that one sentence was enough to give him a week's worth of X-rated dreams. She could have given him a well-deserved, angry dig, or said something meaningless and conventional, but she'd chosen to be honest instead.

I won't lie to your grandfather, she'd told him the first day he was back. A pang of conscience furrowed his forehead. He'd set her up so that she at least had to hide the truth, if not outright lie. Maybe he deserved to walk the plank.

His steps slowed in front of the *Spiritos*, and he realized that his intention to go back to the house hadn't translated itself to his feet. Exasperated, he glanced back toward the *Dolphin*. The light in the galley went out.

But Maria's light was still on, and Maria was still inside the cabin, and he was standing on the dock clutching a bag of coffee as if it were a gift. "I guess you can get out the plank," he muttered toward Miguel's boat.

Another light went on in *Spiritos*'s cabin before the door opened and Maria, in white nightgown and long, flowered robe, stood framed in the cabin's illumination, peering out at him.

"Jake?"

There was a sudden, sharp silence in the darkness, then his answer. "Yes." He stepped down to the catwalk and swung himself over the rail, then crossed the deck toward her, his steps slow and a little diffident. "I have a delivery for the galley." He presented her with the coffee as he stopped in front of her.

She glanced from his face to the bag. "We're not out of coffee."

"I know."

The wind gusted around them, snatching at Maria's robe. Wordlessly she stepped back to let him in. He went by her, and she closed the door, turning to face him.

The cabin glowed with warm yellow light and smelled faintly of the wet wind off the harbor. "I . . . needed an excuse to talk to Miguel. Borrowing five pounds of coffee was what came to mind."

"Oh." Several emotions washed across her face. "Yes, I understand," she said quietly.

A muscle twitched in his jaw. "I had no choice but to . . . deliver it."

The suggestion of a smile touched her mouth. "I doubt Miguel will ask me to account for five pounds of coffee, but if he does, I can tell him it's here."

"If you like, I'll throw the day's supply overboard—make what I told your cousin true."

She crossed her arms, tucking her hands into the folds of her robe. "I don't think you need to resort to pollution of the harbor, Captain Marlow."

"I could feed it to Joaquim tomorrow."

"Feed it to Joaquim?"

"Yeah. But a fifty-ton whale on a caffeine jag might be more awesome than anyone wants to witness. He might start singing like Springsteen. Really rocking out."

"If he does, get it on tape."

He laughed, pushing his hands into his pockets. "Absolutely. But somehow, Sea Sprite, I doubt that Joaquim will ever sing for me. He'll wait for the real captain."

She dropped her gaze, but a tinge of heat crept into her face. "Did you learn anything . . . talking to Miguel?"

He let out a long breath. "Yeah," he said wryly. "I learned you have three brothers and five cousins, and they all believe in dire penalties for the seduction and abandonment of Santos women."

"Oh." She smiled. "Well, you're probably safe. I don't think delivering a bag of coffee constitutes seduction and abandonment."

"I don't know, Sea Sprite." His smile faded, and he met her gaze with serious blue eyes. "I can't seem to think past the seduction part."

There was another silence between them, filled with the tension of awareness as high keyed and sharp as sonar.

Maria felt it all along her nerve endings, an energized, invisible current humming with the closing of a switch left open when she'd walked away from him two hours earlier.

His gaze had slipped down to the white lace edging of her nightgown. The neckline was as modest as anything she owned, but Jake's look made her intensely aware that she was dressed, however modestly, for bed. That her white cotton nightgown could be slipped off by loosening a few buttons. That she wore nothing underneath it.

She closed her eyes, admitting that she would like nothing better than for Jake Marlow to make love to her. To slip off her nightgown, to touch her the way he had on the beach . . .

She gripped the folds of her robe tightly enough to feel the tension in her knuckles. "It won't happen, Jake," she said, but her voice was uncertain, and the words had no more conviction than a shifting sand bar.

He waited for her to open her eyes before he answered her. "Because you don't want it?"

"What I want to have happen," she said, searching for the words, "is for you to finish your investigation, satisfy yourself that no one is committing any crimes, and go back to your insurance agency and leave everything—the fleet, the work, my job—exactly as it was before you came here. That's what I want."

"Yeah." There was a twist to his voice. "Well, life's full of surprises."

"You mean deceit, deliberate accidents . . . sabotage?"

He raked a hand through his hair. "Maybe life will surprise *me* and the accidents will turn out to be just accidents, Sea Sprite. No crime, no enemies."

"Would that be such a surprise, Jake—no enemies?"

"Maybe I'm willing to admit it's possible," he said slowly. "There have been other surprises since I came here."

There had been for her too. She looked at her feet, willing her pulse to slow, willing herself not to be moved by the evidence that Jake wasn't as hard and unchangeable a man as he claimed to be. But he wasn't. She knew it. He was a better man than he thought he was. More caring. More honest, despite his deceptions.

Outside the cabin the first hard front of rain hit the boat, drumming on the wooden deck. He glanced up, listening, then looked back to her. "Your whale's been coming to the boat," he said.

"I know."

"I think he must recognize the sound of the engine."

"Yes—I told you he did."

"I know. But I can't get over the idea that he's coming for you, not the boat."

Her mouth curved slightly at the corners. "Why couldn't he be coming for you?"

"Right," Jake said, with a dry chuckle. "He's waiting for Miguel and the rest of your cousins to throw me overboard. It . . . occurred to me on the way here that you might want me dumped in the bay. You might be angry enough to do it yourself."

"No," she said softly, "I'm not angry enough for that."

He rubbed the bridge of his nose between thumb and forefinger and started to say something, but she spoke before he could.

"I was angry because I come from a family where trust is taken for granted, Jake. I'm not very good at . . . diplomacy. Maybe you were right. I'm naïve. But I didn't suspect that a few minor accidents were evidence of crimes. I can't suspect Miguel of sabotaging the Marlow boats and betraying the man he works for. And I didn't suspect that you had a . . . an undercover mission either."

He dropped his hand from his face. "That was your mistake," he said flatly. "Trusting me."

She searched his face, but couldn't read his expression.

"You trust too easily, Sea Sprite. I would think you would have learned that, working for my grandfather."

"That's not what I've learned." He frowned at her,

and she lifted her chin. Some instinct told her the cynicism she heard so often in his voice wasn't part of Jake's nature. He'd acquired it somewhere along the way, a protection, like his grandfather's antagonism, like her own hurt anger.

"Is that what your divorce was about, Jake?" she asked softly. "You couldn't trust each other?"

She thought for a moment he wasn't going to answer, then he gave a huff of humorless laughter and shoved his hands forcefully into his pockets. "Not quite," he said. "She was doing the books for the business. Unfortunately I never bothered to check her figures, even when I knew the marriage was shaky. I should have." His smile was wry. "My grandfather pointed that out to me more than once."

"He was wrong to tell you that. He was wrong to think that—that trust is foolish. And you were wrong to listen to him."

The wind gusted, fierce and angry with the power of the spring storm. "I don't think so," Jake said. "He was trying to tell me all relationships are governed by self-interest." His voice dropped, and the flint-blue Marlow gaze swung around her small cabin, then fixed on her face again. "We're talking about human relationships here, not whales."

It was a dig, but the sting was taken out of it by her understanding of Wyatt. Deliberately she unclenched her fist from the folds of her robe and let it drop to her side. "We *were* talking about whales, though," she said.

His voice, when he spoke, was even more quiet than hers. "I'm not the sort of man who listens to whale songs, Sea Sprite. Don't fool yourself about that."

His gaze was so intense she felt it all the way to the pit of her stomach, where flutters of sensuality sent melting warmth spreading outward. But the warning voice in the back of her mind that told her he was right, she shouldn't trust him, had set a tight band of tension along her shoulder blades. She tipped her head down and massaged the back of her neck with one hand. Her hair was caught in a loose coil at her nape. Sighing, she ran her fingers through it, then shook her head to loosen it.

When she looked up, Jake's eyes had darkened to something more than intensity, and she felt the heat of it as if she had just drawn close to an open flame. Startled, she made a small sound, barely more than a breath. Her gaze was caught in Jake's as if she were mesmerized by the sudden, hot current of sensuality that ran between them.

She knew what the touch of his hands would feel like, the heat of his mouth, the hard, masculine strength of his body. Her own body was already warming, yielding, yearning. His gaze flicked to her mouth, and her lips parted in unconscious response and invitation, as if he were already close enough to kiss her.

He didn't move, only looked at her, and for the space of a few heartbeats Maria's half-dazed mind wavered between going to him or waiting for him to come to her.

Three seconds later the deck jolted beneath her feet, and the *Spiritos* shuddered into a skid as a high-pitched, agonized groan of metal on wood shrieked into the cabin. Maria's reality shattered, then coalesced into frightening focus: They'd been rammed by one hundred tons of steel hull.

Seven

Maria was across the cabin before the boat stopped shuddering. The door crashed against the outside wall as she flung it open. She slid, barefoot, on the wet deck, around the front of the wheelhouse, clinging to the doorframe.

"Maria!" Jake shouted behind her. She felt his hand grip her shoulder, then he swore volubly at the sight that confronted them.

The *Dolphin's* hull loomed over the deck of the *Spiritos*, where the big boat's stern had swung around, pivoting on a single line still tied at the bow. Incredulity and shock raced through Maria as she took in the accident. How could the *Dolphin* have come loose from three lines? The catwalk between the two boats was slanted, half submerged between them as the *Dolphin*, moved by the force of the wind, rode over the flimsy barrier as if it were so much seaweed. The *Spiritos* groaned again as the big boat scraped along her rail.

Maria turned, wrenching away from Jake's hand, glancing around her. The *Spiritos's* boarding ramp was half submerged with the catwalk, unusable. The *Dolphin's* stern was too far above the smaller boat to be reached from the deck.

She sprinted for the bow and swung herself over the rail, dropping to the dock far below the tide-lifted *Spiritos*. Jake's shout followed her. She was already running when he thudded onto the dock.

"Maria!" There was more, but he was shouting into the wind, and she couldn't make out the words.

The *Dolphin* had swept diagonally across its slip, held by one straining bowline. The line had already pulled high on the piling to which it had been tied.

Jake's voice, directly behind her, was as tense as the straining line. "How the *hell* did this happen?"

The three ropes that should have held the *Dolphin* secure in the slip hung loose over her gunwales, dangling into the water as if they'd never been tied to the pilings. The wind gusted again, and in front of them the bowline tautened. The high-pitched groan of the rubbing boats grated on Maria's nerves as if she, not her boat, were taking the punishment.

"I'll call the harbormaster," Jake said, close to her ear. "And we'll get some extra bumpers out here."

"How are we going to get them on?" she demanded. "The *Dolphin*'s jammed up against her! And the tide's going to turn. It'll be worse."

Jake's mouth tightened, but he had no answer. "We need some help here—"

"The harbormaster won't get here for half an hour! What if the line doesn't hold? You want the *Dolphin* loose in the harbor?"

"The line'll hold," he said harshly. "And we're insured, dammit."

The bitterness in his voice added determination to her own desperate urgency. "Watch the knot on this line," she ordered.

"Don't touch that!"

But she'd already reached as far out as she could on

the remaining bow line and stepped off the dock.

"Maria!"

She didn't look back. Jake, she knew, wouldn't take his eyes off the line as long as she was counting on him. She swung herself hand over hand along the rope, her robe and nightgown fluttering around her feet. The line payed out over a metal guard below the *Dolphin*'s railing. She grabbed the lower crossbar of the rail and pulled herself up and over it, onto the deck.

Jake's eyes were glued to her when she glanced across at him. The tension in his body communicated itself to her even in the wind and the darkness, but she didn't stop to analyze what it meant. Turning to look down the length of the boat, she saw that the stern cleat still held a loop of rope. She sprinted along the deck, then leaned over the rail to haul the wet line from the water.

She coiled the rope, hauled back, and heaved the line into the wind. It fell far short of the dock, splashing into the harbor. Frustrated, she leaned to haul it in again, her toes dug into the deck for purchase.

"Get closer!" Jake was gesturing at her. She nodded, understanding, and moved down the railing amidships, where the *Dolphin* was closer to the dock. Jake leaned out from the dock as she heaved the heavy, wet line again, but as she let it go, the wind gusted toward her, and the line dropped into the water. There was another squeal of wood against metal from the lee side of the big boat.

Maria's teeth clenched together, and she felt tears of desperation sting her eyes. She leaned toward the wet rope, but before she reached it, a splash from the dock snapped her head up.

Jake had dived into the harbor after the rope. She

watched him swim for it. He grasped the heavy end of the line before it sank completely, and started back toward the dock.

"Oh, Jake. Bless you," she murmured.

He got up onto the dock, leaned over for a moment, catching his breath, then braced one foot against the piling and started hauling on the rope. Slowly, inch by inch, the *Dolphin* swung back parallel to her slip.

She could almost feel the *Spiritos* sigh in relief. The *Dolphin* swung steadily back as Jake pulled on the rope, letting up as she moved into place, and making the line fast before the wind pulled the stern taut against the line.

It was only a matter of minutes to secure all of the boat's four heavy lines, but by the time it was done, Maria was shivering. She pulled her wet robe around her, cold and shaking from delayed reaction. Her feet felt like ice on the metal deck. Jake had leaned against a piling, his clothes plastered against him in the wind. He must be even colder than she.

Letting out a long breath, she walked around to the *Dolphin*'s boarding ramp. The catwalk had righted itself, wet but floating normally, and she let herself down to it. There was no visible damage to the *Spiritos* except scraped paint. A closer look would have to wait until morning.

Jake was standing on the dock when she reached it, holding out his hand to her, but one glance at his face told her he was furious. She took his hand with no comment and let him help her up to the dock. "Jake, thank—"

"What the hell did you think you were doing?" he shouted before she could get the words out. "That damn line could have come loose!"

The force of his anger was enough to give off physical heat. "No, it couldn't," she said. "You were watching it."

"How the hell do you know? You didn't bother to look back."

She stared at him, taken aback by his unexpected reaction. "The *Dolphin* could have been halfway across the harbor by now! Instead she's safe in her slip because we got her there!"

"So I'm supposed to be grateful you—"

"No," she snapped. "*I'm* supposed to be. I'm the manager of this fleet, and I'm not going to lose a boat because of some unjustifiable carelessness in tying her up."

"That's what you think this was? Carelessness?" She was silenced.

"Who the hell around here doesn't know how to make a line fast? The mates? Miguel?"

She shivered again and pulled her robe closer around her. "The wind's strong. And it's an unusually high tide, and . . ." There wasn't enough conviction in her words to finish the sentence. She glanced toward the *Dolphin,* her lower lip caught in her teeth.

"An accident?" he said with enough sarcasm to make her look back at him. "My God, you're not naïve enough to believe that. Use your head."

Stung, she lashed out at him. "What's so logical about believing someone tried to destroy the *Dolphin*? It's not even a good way to destroy a boat. The *Dolphin* could have come through it just fine. And anyway, you said yourself—the boats are insured."

"The boats are, but not the Marlow fleet's reputation. It wouldn't do much for our business if we carelessly lost one of our boats on a windy night, would it?"

She stared at him, blinking into the rain, trying to

reject the idea, but in truth she couldn't. Jake was right. No one who worked for the fleet would have been careless in securing the *Dolphin* on a night like this. It was difficult even to believe that Miguel could have left the boat without noticing something amiss. Someone had to have been very quick, or very clever . . . and as criminal as Jake Marlow believed.

She swallowed hard, wondering if cynicism was catching. "Well, then, I'd think you'd be glad I did something to save the Marlow fleet's reputation."

He reached for her so fast, she didn't have time to react. His hands closed around her shoulders, hard enough to hurt and strong enough to lift her to her toes. "This fleet doesn't need you taking chances with your life. Do you understand that?"

Shocked again by the force of his anger, she stared at him, her eyes wide. A muscle clenched at the side of his jaw, then he let out a long breath. His grip on her shoulders loosened, but he didn't let her go.

"I've been around boats all my life, Jake," she said. "I know what I can do. I wasn't taking that much of a chance."

"You tell someone to watch a rope and then you jump for it like this is a circus? If it had slipped, you would have hit the side of the hull like a trap line."

There was another emotion behind his anger that she recognized, and she puzzled it out in dawning realization. "I knew you'd watch the rope," she said quietly.

She felt the tension of his hands gripping her upper arms again, echoed by the intensity in his eyes as he returned her gaze. Something passed between them that went beyond words understood or implied. Something that needed to be said another way . . .

She closed her eyes for a moment, reaching for control. "I want to check the other boats, Jake," she said finally.

He nodded, then, a few seconds later, released her. "I'm going to talk to my grandfather." There was a grim note in the statement, and she let it pass without comment.

Abruptly he turned toward the house and walked away from her. She watched him go, unaware of her cold feet, her damp nightclothes, or her threatened fleet. He didn't once turn around, or hesitate, or even run a hand through his wet hair. She had only that one look and her own imagination to tell her he felt anything for her besides anger. And her imagination had been out of hand for days now, since he'd almost made love to her on Joaquim's beach.

Hands jammed into his pockets, eyes on the dock in front of him, Jake made himself put one foot in front of the other, walking away from her. When he'd grabbed her by the shoulders he'd shaken her robe open. Her white cotton nightgown was damp enough to be transparent—a tantalizing image of innocence and suggestion that had him so hot, he could imagine his wet clothes steaming with the kind of fire that burned from the inside out.

If he hadn't let go of her, he would have pulled her against him, sealed her mouth with his, and brought her with him down to the wet dock, and the hell with everything else.

Right, Marlow. Everything else but your own needs.

He clenched his teeth even harder as an ache he didn't understand shot through him. That was what he'd done since the first time he'd met her. Forgotten everything but his own need. It was what he'd done tonight. He knew he'd been holding her too roughly, shaking her when he should have been comforting her, but she hadn't protested, hadn't paid back his irrational anger with her own.

I knew you'd watch the rope.

He stopped for a moment, feeling a band of tension across his chest.

What was it about this woman that turned his guts inside out? Every encounter he'd had with her had made him feel like the worst kind of heel. But staying away from her was worse. The innocent trust and ancient wisdom she managed to project in equal measures had him spinning like a top.

She'd been shivering, he remembered. He should have held her, walked her back to her boat, and wrapped her in three wool blankets, but he knew if he touched her, it wouldn't be blankets he'd be wrapping around her. It wouldn't be comfort he was offering. And he doubted he would have made it to the boat.

Angry with himself, everything he could name, and a host of things he couldn't, Jake stalked in through the front door of his grandfather's house. He let it bang shut behind him . . . then stopped where he was. The house was dark, silent, obviously asleep for the night. He felt a quick, irrational surge of anger at his grandfather for leaving Maria to face the *Dolphin*'s crisis on her own, then suppressed it, frowning at himself. What the hell did he have to be angry about? Maria was manager of the fleet. She was the one who was supposed to face any crisis that arose and do whatever it took to solve the problem.

That was her job. Whether Jake liked it or not.

He let out a long breath and slumped back against the door. If he'd come there with the idea of convincing

Wyatt that it was time to involve the police, he was on a pointless errand. The only person who could accomplish that was Maria herself.

After she'd risked her neck to save the *Dolphin*, checked the lines on all the other boats, and dealt with any immediate damage to the *Spiritos*, if there was any.

Was there? She hadn't said there was. She would have mentioned it if she needed help, wouldn't she? Or would she have assumed it was her responsibility, like everything else?

Swearing under his breath, Jake stripped off his wet jacket, pulled on the first dry one he touched in the hall closet, and let himself out again.

The Marlow dock was deserted, the big boats secure in their slips, no sign of any problems with the moorings. The rain had stopped as suddenly as it had started. Jake boarded the *Porpoise*, walked through her, then checked each of the other boats before he made his way along the dock to the *Spiritos*.

The cabin was dark. The boat looked, like the others, deserted, secured at the end of the dock. Maybe Maria had gone up to the house for some coffee and a hot bath, and he'd missed her while he was on one of the boats. He couldn't stop the bite of disappointment, even while a more logical part of his mind was telling him it would be better all around if she had gone up to the house. Being alone with her was no more logical an idea than it had been five minutes ago. But his logic had been on hold all night long.

He boarded the *Spiritos*, checking automatically for damage as he stepped over her rail. He noticed nothing except scraped paint. *Spiritos*, for all her sleek, beautiful lines, was as strong as her work required.

She'd withstood wind and rough seas before that night. Probably more than she should have, with Maria at the wheel, chasing whales.

He wondered if she turned off the marine radio when she was listening to the hydrophone, and he bit back the irritation that came with the thought. Maria was an excellent navigator, as familiar with the navigational aids on the instrument board as anyone he knew. But the day they'd gone out looking for her whale, she'd been navigating by something other than radar and radio. His mouth quirked at one corner in self-deprecating understanding. Maria Santos worked on some kind of instinct that was hard to believe, and even harder to resist. Jake had been drawn in more surely than the whale. There could have been hurricane warnings blaring over the airwaves, and he doubted he would have been aware of anything except that he wanted Maria Santos like hell on fire.

And he hadn't stopped wanting her since. He made a harsh sound and walked toward the forward deck, sucking in his breath sharply as the wind gusted around the front of the wheelhouse and slapped his wet slacks against his legs. Like the fifty-degree water she'd gotten him into twice now, the wind wasn't quite cold enough to cool off his X-rated thoughts.

He swore to himself, jammed his hands into the pockets of his jacket, and turned back toward the cabin.

Maria was on the deck, sitting cross-legged under the overhang of the wheelhouse with her back against the cabin, her white nightgown tucked improbably into a pair of jeans, a big sleeping bag wrapped around her shoulders.

He stopped dead. "What are you doing there?"

She smiled. "I'm the owner. I belong here. *You're* the hijacker."

The idea that she let herself be so vulnerable made him, for no good reason, angry once again. "You figure you'd let me take off with the boat before you said anything?"

Her eyebrows rose slightly at his tone of voice. "I knew it was you, Jake."

"How?"

"I recognized your footsteps."

"My *footsteps*?"

"Did you talk to your grandfather?"

"No."

Water slapped rhythmically against the hull of the boat. The *Spiritos* listed against her lines as the wind tugged at her. Maria shivered and pulled the sleeping bag closer.

Jake stood where he was and fought the temptation to get closer to her, offer her his jacket, wrap her in his arms. Sitting in the shadows, she looked like some fragile boat-spirit conjured up from the wind and the water, in need of careful nurturing to keep her from returning to the sea.

"I came down to see if there was any damage to the *Spiritos*," he said finally.

"I don't think there was much harm done. But . . . thanks."

A cold blast of wind cut across the deck. Jake hunched his shoulders in his jacket.

"I'll make some coffee," Maria said, moving to push aside the sleeping bag.

Coffee. Every time he saw her, she offered him coffee. And then they went on to something more intimate. The thought provoked a response so immediate, he clenched his hands into fists. "No. Don't bother." The words were more short than he intended, and he bit back a frustration that threatened to tear him apart. "Look. Why don't you go up to the house and get some sleep in a warm bed? You've checked out all the boats."

"I think I should be out here tonight."

"I'll stay here. I can sleep on the *Spiritos*. Or the *Dolphin*."

She was silent, then said, "Thank you. But I have to stay anyway. It's my job. I'm responsible for anything that happens . . . and what we do next."

Jake set his jaw against a raw sound of need that rose at the image his mind conjured.

That wasn't what she meant, Marlow.

But maybe if you touched her, you could make it what she meant.

He jammed his hands into his pockets, his mouth set in a hard line. "Fine," he snapped. "Do you want me to sleep on the *Dolphin*?"

There was a long and assessing silence, then, with a small, graceful gesture she shrugged off the sleeping bag and stood up.

Jake's muscles went rigid.

She clasped her hands around her elbows, hugging her bare arms close to her body. The wind gusted, and the fragile cotton nightgown contoured her body, rounded against the swell of her breast, dimpled over her puckered nipple. She stood still for a moment, ignoring the wind, then walked toward him. Two steps brought her in front of him. Her gaze dropped from his eyes to his mouth, then to the heavy, driven pulse in his throat.

She reached with one hand to touch the back of his neck, then rose on her toes and brushed her lips against his.

He didn't move until her mouth touched his, then he gave a muffled groan and pulled her savagely against him, one hand around the back of her head, the other arm clamped around her waist as if they were locked in a savage struggle. But there was no struggle. Her mouth opened to the exploring penetration of his tongue, and she allowed the hard, primitive claiming of his kiss as if the sudden, rough intimacy were as natural as the wind.

When Jake lifted his mouth from hers, she was staring at him, eyes wide, lips parted, her gaze steady. He was trembling, his body coursing with raw, savage heat, wanting her more than he wanted to breathe. "You'd better think about where you want me to sleep, Sea Sprite," he said, the words a low growl.

"I have thought about it," she murmured. "Every night since you got here. The time for thinking about it is over."

Eight

Maria knew the moment he took in the meaning of her words. His fingers gentled on the back of her head, and the desperate, rough band of his arm around her waist loosened. The desperation remained only in his voice. "Maria, don't make any mistakes about me. Don't fool yourself into—"

She touched his face, and he stopped talking.

His eyes burned into hers with an intensity that registered as heat. "You'd better be sure. Because once I start, I don't think—"

"So don't think."

The hard resistance of his will, his false anger, turned like the vertex of the tide. He swallowed, and his eyes shut for a moment.

She let herself smile. "For a marauding pirate, you're awfully slow at raping and pillaging."

A warm rush of breath fanned her face as he expelled it. "What do you know about raping and pillaging, Sea Sprite?"

"Not much."

His hands left her back to frame the sides of her face. His thumbs just touched her cheekbones, the movement as delicate and careful as the trembling of a compass needle. "No. I didn't think so."

She shivered, and her whispered voice was husky. "But I suppose I could tell you how to start."

"Oh, yes, Sea Sprite. Tell me how to start."

She put her hands over his, running her fingers along the wide knuckles, then touching her palms to the back of his hands. "I want you to kiss me again."

He brought his mouth down on hers with slow, deliberate care, sliding his lips against hers in a kiss as gentle as the last one had been demanding. The exquisite, light touch of his mouth caressed and promised, without the slightest hint of force, though beneath her hands she could feel the tension in his wrist and corded forearms. His lips were warm, alive, sensate, and she was all the more aware of the intimacy as she slipped her arms around his cool, waterproof jacket. His mouth lingered on hers in leisurely, unhurried sensitivity, barely brushing her lips, moving just enough to taste and caress, as if he were absorbing some essence too fragile for force.

Through the fine cotton of her nightgown she could feel the smooth surface of his jacket against her breasts. One of his long, muscled legs pressed against hers, and she could feel moisture from his slacks seeping through her jeans, touching her skin through the layer of cloth like the promise of intimacy.

She shivered, moving closer to him, wanting more. When he lifted his head and gazed down at her, her lips stayed parted. "Like that?" he murmured.

"No. Like a pirate." She smiled. "Like nothing will stop you from having your way with me."

"Nothing could stop me except you, Sea Sprite," he said, close to her mouth. "And if you won't . . ." His mouth touched her again, traced the contour of her upper lip, then he shifted his head to cover her lips with his, and she felt the sudden, masterful pressure of demand and claim. His tongue probed the opening of her lips, then filled the feminine warmth of her mouth with forceful, possessive exploration that left her trembling and breathless.

His hands moved to her shoulders, her back, the hollow above the back waistband of her jeans. He wrapped her up, pulled her against him, held her captive for a kiss that demanded surrender.

Spiritos quivered beneath their feet, straining against her lines, and Maria felt an echoing reverberation through her whole body, as heat hammered in her chest and her pulse thrummed in her ears. There was no thought, no logic, no power she could remember to combat the sweet aching Jake stirred in her body. She met his tongue with her own, matching the sensual, gliding, arousing patterns with the ardent response of a primitive, ritual dance.

Both of them were breathing raggedly when he broke the seal of their kiss and trailed hot, damp sensation along her jaw to the sensitive cord of her neck just below her ear. She thought the wind shook the *Spiritos* again, but it might have been his breath in her ear and her own response to it.

Oh, but he was good. As good as he'd been at flirting, at teasing, at kissing her that first afternoon in the cafeteria, when her world had shivered beneath her feet and her thoughts had homed on him like seabirds to their nesting place. "Jake Marlow," she murmured, nuzzling her cheek against his.

He murmured something incoherent, but it was enough. He wanted her. She knew it from the first time he'd touched her, from the honesty of his pursuit, from the words that warned her away. Despite the subterfuge of his purpose there, he had an emotional honesty she'd trusted from the first, she realized. She trusted now, putting her body in his hands, setting her emotions free to wrap them both in the warmth of sensual expression.

His strong hands sculpted her back, contoured her hips, caressed the curve of her buttocks. He pulled her against his hips, and through the wet fabric of his chinos she felt the honest evidence of his desire. His hips made slow, circling movements, and she followed them with her own, moving in cadence to the rhythm of desire he set.

She was going to make love to him. She knew that. She had known it before she started, but the sudden realization stopped her heart for a second. She shivered once more and felt his arms close around her.

"Maria," he murmured, his voice husky. "We can go in. Or back to the house—or someplace else. Anywhere you want." She felt his smile. "Boston. New York. Bermuda. Atlantis."

Her breath was half laughter. "No. Here."

"Here?" There was a disbelieving chuckle in the word.

"Yes." He had lifted his head to see her face, and she smiled, watching the bemused expression in his eyes. "Here. On deck. On the *Spiritos*."

He gave a huff of disbelieving laughter. "On your sleeping bag?"

"Yes. On my sleeping bag. On the deck. On the water." She slid her fingers around his neck, into the thick, straight hair at the back of his head, and pulled his head down to her again. "You belong on the water, Jake Marlow," she murmured against his lips. "Sailing the seven seas."

"Mm. In search of treasure." He walked her backward toward the overhang of the cabin where she'd

been sitting, kissing her while they moved. His damp thighs nudged against hers in slow, deliberate movements that brought her hips into intimate contact with the lower part of his body. When the pile of quilted nylon rustled against the back of her ankles, Jake stopped. His hands slid down over her jeans to her thighs, and he lifted her until she straddled him. He held her against him while his hips rocked forward and his tongue invaded her open mouth repeatedly, echoing the rhythm of the joining they would make with their bodies.

She clung to him, seeking the heat and strength of him against her stomach, her breasts, her inner thighs. A rising tide of desire drove her closer, closer than she could get, until she was clinging to him with legs and arms and returning the kiss with passion that equaled his.

Jake bent into a crouch, so that she was sitting on his lap, and he leaned to reach behind her and arrange the sleeping bag. Still kissing her, he duck-walked her, one lurching step at a time, toward the outside storage locker, where she'd left a folded blanket. His mouth slipped away from hers when he bent her half backward to reach for the blanket.

Laughing, clinging to his shoulders, she asked what he was doing.

"Showing you . . ." He teetered on one foot and snatched. He shook out the blanket behind him, shaking her as well, then a cloak of wool covered her shoulders.

"What? Your nefarious intentions?"

"Yeah. Pirates do this all the time." As if to demonstrate the truth of the statement, he lifted her easily off his lap and set her down on the sleeping bag. One hand on her shoulder pressed her down onto her back, and he followed, lying beside her, his arm cradling her head.

She had a glimpse of black sky pricked with emerging stars before Jake's head blotted it out, and he laid his hand against her cheek. She raised her face for his kiss, touching his shoulder, but he didn't kiss her. Instead he caught her hand in his own and brought it around to his throat. He pressed her palm flat against his chest and guided it down to his belt, then lower, to the hard ridge of flesh beneath the zipper of his chinos.

"My intentions are nefarious enough for fifty years of raping and pillaging, Sea Sprite," he muttered in a rough whisper.

She smiled, shaping her hand to him, measuring and learning with slow, sensual strokes. "I suppose that means you'll start soon, then?"

His breath hissed out through his teeth, though she heard the grin in the sound. He moved her hand away. "Very soon if you do that again."

Laughter bubbled through her, rippling sensual excitement all through her body. She felt light as air, suspended over a vast ocean of sensuality, set free as a dolphin in a vast ocean.

Jake's hand skimmed up her hip and flattened on her nightgown, following it up to the curve of her breast. His palm lingered there, making slow, sensitive strokes that just barely brushed the fine cotton against her nipple. She arched her back and turned toward him. He braced himself on his elbows and framed her breasts with both hands, his thumbs on the hollows just above her ribs, his hands gently rubbing the gown to tease the rose-dark crests into hard, aching buds of readiness.

A sigh of longing shivered from her. He lifted her

breasts through the fragile white lawn, then bent his head to the lace edging of her gown, just touching her skin with his lips. "You smell so good, Sea Sprite." His breath heated her skin. "Like cotton and lace and . . . innocence."

He lifted his head, still for a minute, and Maria put her hands over his and slid them up to cover her breasts, pressing against his palms while a small, incoherent sound came from her throat.

He kissed her again, his hands on her breasts, shaping and reshaping her soft flesh while his tongue plundered in welcome assault. Her hands slipped inside his jacket to push it off his shoulders while his went to the button of her jeans and worked it loose. The bunched folds of her nightgown came sliding out of her waistband, then she felt his hand on the skin of her rib cage under the billowing material. She pulled off his jacket.

She reached for the buttons of his damp shirt. "You smell like salt water and seaweed, Captain Marlow," she told him.

He chuckled, helping her with the buttons. "I'm sorry, Sea Sprite. But you keep luring me into the drink."

She laughed again, more from the delight of their intimacy, the rightness of this act, than from any humor in his words. "Mm. I like salt and seaweed." She lifted her head to kiss his chest as he peeled off the shirt, tasting the salt on his skin, smelling the warm, masculine scent of him. His chest was lightly sprinkled with blond hair, soft to her exploring fingers, in contrast to the hard, honed musculature of his shoulders, his ribs, his upper arms. She heard the snap of his pants, and the muffled burr of his zipper, then the blanket moved against her shoulders as he slithered out of the wet pants, tossed them behind him onto the deck, and pulled the blanket over his hips.

His palm skimmed over her hip, her leg, then up along her inner thigh, and stopped there, brushing back over the wet denim. Her jeans were as damp as his pants had been. She unzipped them and lifted her hips. Jake pulled the denim down around her knees. She worked her feet free and kicked the jeans out of their way.

"Wait a minute." He reached behind her, toward the discarded clothes. "I need my wallet."

She put her hand on his shoulder. "No."

He glanced back at her, frowning quizzically, and she smiled. "I've taken care of it."

He pulled his arm back slowly, watching her face while a slow smile of comprehension spread over his features. "And you're . . ."

"Yes." With one bare foot she caressed the side of his leg, delighting in the strong texture of muscled calf, the dip at the back of his knee, the soft hair on his hard thigh.

His warm hands curved around her hipbones, and his thumbs explored the hollows at the sides of her stomach, where the bottom of her nightgown gathered in creased folds below her waist. She waited, one knee raised, her foot on his thigh, for his hands to close the one remaining gap of intimacy, to touch her at the most sensitive core of her femininity. Instead he fell still, only his thumbs moving in slow, sensual circles on her stomach.

"Your skin is so smooth," he murmured. "Like the inside of a shell. Like abalone."

His long fingers moved, brushing up under her gown along her rib cage, baring her skin to the faintly cool shadows under their tented blanket. The cloth skimmed over her breasts as he raised the nightgown, and she lifted her arms for him to take it off, impatient for his touch again.

The warm, wet caress of his mouth and tongue followed his hands. He kissed the cleft between her breasts, drawing a whimper of longing from her throat.

"And you smell even better than your nightgown," he murmured against her. "Like spring wind. Like home. Like something a man would dream about coming home to."

He nuzzled her breast, stroking with lips and tongue, spreading hot, cascading shivers out along her body, fingertips to toes. When he drew the beaded peak into his mouth, she gave a low moan of response and clung to him while a quiver of sensation vibrated in the center of her being.

His palm swathed a wide trail down her stomach. When he touched her, finally, she was burning for him, aching with a need that took her voice away. With utmost tenderness he moved over her, stroking, caressing, learning her, and her breath sighed out in an aching rush of desire.

"Yes, Sea Sprite. Burn for me, the way I do for you. The way I want you. The way I've wanted you for days . . ."

She moved under him, reaching for him, guiding him toward her. "Come home, then," she murmured on a breath that was half whisper, half sigh.

His homing was slow, strong, as natural as the surging tide. When he slid his hands under her buttocks and lifted her to sheathe himself deep within her, she called out his name, more than once. Then the night, the stars, the cloth-padded deck beneath them receded into a cadence of sound: their breath, the whisper of wind, the murmur of water, the shared, silent song of communion that governed the joining of their bodies. He murmured her name, the names he used for her, each one an endearment she heard in her body as much as in his voice as the rhythm of their movements matched and harmonized.

She clung to him, her breathing ragged as he stroked her body past the point of thought, took her soul beyond awareness of itself, each beat building to a cadence of music drawn out in unbearable pleasure. Then, together, they spilled over the edge. The sound that came from his throat was indecipherable, but she knew the meaning, and she echoed it.

When it was over and they'd drifted to the surface, sated and released, their muscles limp, Jake barely found the energy to shift his weight off her slight body and roll to his hip, taking her with him. With one limp gesture he reached for the blanket and tugged it over their shoulders, then wrapped her again in his arms to savor the rich, heavy peace of aftermath, barely aware of the outside world.

Jake's only thought as he held her against him, listening to the drift of water and wind and his own satisfaction, was that the *Spiritos* rested easily in her slip, the wind no longer pulling at her. The tide had turned. It would slip out during the night, without their help, marking off their time together. He pulled her closer. He couldn't hold back the tide, but he could give them other ways of marking it.

Jake awoke with sharp, brilliant sunlight on his face. The deck was rolling gently beneath his naked backside, and the *Spiritos*'s engines thrummed. There was nothing around the boat but water.

Once again, he realized, Maria Santos had swept all his assumptions out from under him. This time she'd done it literally.

Grinning, he ran a hand through his hair, wondering if this particular morning-after scenario violated his ideas of appropriate control of his life. Before he'd finished the thought, he knew he didn't give a damn what the answer was.

He could smell coffee coming from the small cabin, rich and aromatic. He was hungry. For food, for the day, for Maria.

He stood up and went looking for her.

She was at the counter in the small cabin, her back to him, folding a blanket. She was dressed, minimally, in cutoff chinos and a bathing-suit top. Her hair was a loose, dark cloud over her shoulders, as it had been all night. She reached above her toward the locker, graceful, efficient, feminine. The stirring in his body was almost instantaneous. Maybe real men didn't get kidnapped and wake up naked in borrowed sleeping bags, he thought wryly, but his manhood didn't seem to be having any trouble with it.

He leaned a hip against the doorway and waited for her to turn around.

When she did, she stopped where she was, surprised, wide-eyed. Her gaze slipped down over him, and color rose in her cheeks.

He scowled at her to keep an idiotic, absurdly pleased grin from breaking over his face. "Where the hell are we?"

"Out to sea."

"I figured that much out for myself. From all the water."

"We're almost at the Bank."

He squeezed his eyes shut, ran his hand through

his hair again, and looked at her. Her skin, in the sunny light from the portholes, looked golden, glowing, translucent as candle flame. He could feel it as if he were touching her—silk over willow wood, giving back his touch as gracefully as water.

"Want some coffee?" she asked.

He pushed himself away from the door, crossed the small cabin, and reached behind her for the cup she'd half finished. He drank a mouthful, watching her, then put the cup down and tipped her face up to kiss her. Wrapping his arm around her shoulders, he pulled her against him, nestling her between his thighs. He slid his hands into the back of her shorts and encountered no underwear. He kept his hand there, against her warm skin, making sure their bodies were touching.

"Almost at the Bank?" he muttered. "How'd I sleep through all that?"

Her shoulders lifted and dropped, casual. "Under the sleeping bag. It's pretty heavy. You can't hear much under there."

His hand slid over the curve of her buttock. Possessiveness flared through him, as it had in the night. "I know." He nuzzled the side of her neck. She made a soft sound of response, satisfying, needed. He ran his lips along the edge of her jaw.

"I wanted to be out on the water with you," she said softly.

He smiled. "I would have helped. You didn't have to kidnap me. Who cast off?"

She hesitated, not so much in measurable time as in the slight tensing of her body. "Miguel," she said. "He was there early."

There was a beat of silence. "Miguel?"

She gave a laugh, edged with awkwardness. "He didn't know you were there. It was just like a pile of disorderly sleeping bags. I was hoping you wouldn't wake up and destroy my reputation." Her smile faded as Jake studied her face.

"Miguel? He was back there this morning?"

"Yes. But that's not unusual. He's often there early, to check on the *Dolphin.*"

Jake's mouth tightened, and his hands, unconsciously, moved on her back, holding her in the hard, enclosing circle of his arms. "And the *Dolphin did* need checking on, didn't she?"

She ignored the irony. "I told him what happened, Jake."

He squeezed his eyes shut and took a deep breath, making himself absorb the information without overt reaction.

"I wanted to know whether he'd checked those lines himself."

"Right," he muttered. "And did he?"

She met his gaze, then shook her head. "No. Not when he left for the night. He'd checked them earlier, when the *Dolphin* tied up."

Jake's mouth quirked cynically, and his voice had an edge. "Did you fill him in on all the details while you were at it? Did you tell him all about the sabotage?"

She glanced away, then back at him. "Miguel's not guilty of any of that. You *know* people after a while, Jake."

"Maybe *you* do."

"Miguel's worked for the Marlows for years. Far longer than I have. Longer than you have, for that matter."

"And people change sometimes. You can't count

on automatic innocence. You can't count on really knowing people, either, Maria."

She met his gaze, and he could see her weighing their words, coming to her own balance. Her voice was soft when she spoke. "I can."

"You might think you can—"

"I'm the manager of this fleet, Jake. I'll still be running it when your investigation is over. I'll still be working with the captains, the crews, your grandfather. I owe them some loyalty."

He pulled his hand back from her, pinched the bridge of his nose, then spread his fingertips over his eyes. He didn't want to discuss this, deal with it, let it intrude on the heavy pull of sensuality that drew him to Maria.

Yet what she said was true, as much as what he'd said. She was connected to the Marlow fleet in ways he was not. She'd still be there when he left.

The thought plunged a sliver of emotion into his gut, not quite identifiable, not quite dismissible.

She'd surprised him again, taken him off balance, knocked him off course. She acted on a value system he couldn't predict and had to struggle to comprehend. Like talking, sometimes, to a different species.

He felt a spurt of reactive anger, knowing it was a senseless protection against his inability to control this situation, this train of events, this woman.

She'd crossed her arms in front of her, hunching her shoulders a little. Her gaze dropped to his naked chest, and a slight wash of color tinted her cheeks, as it had when he'd walked in.

He reached for her, sliding his fingers into the hair at the back of her neck and tipping her face up. Deliberately he brought his mouth down to hers. His kiss was hard, hungry, more dominating than he'd been with her the night before, but her resistance melted almost immediately. She opened her lips with a sigh and put her arms around him, letting him guide her against him.

Still kissing her, he slid his hands around her waist and unsnapped her shorts. They hit the deck with a soft rustle, and Jake's exploring hands claimed all of her bared skin, relearning the texture and shape of her, moving against her in a slow dance of sensual demand until he heard her sigh again.

"Where?" he muttered against her mouth.

"The deck. In the sun."

With one swift motion he swept an arm under her knees and picked her up, then carried her out to the sleeping bag. He lowered her to it. "I wanted you to wake up with me, Sea Sprite. I want to make love to you. I want to spend the day making love to you, until we can't see straight. Until we can't talk. So forget what I said, okay? Forget everything else. For now. For today."

He felt her smile, slow and warm against his chest. "Make me forget, Pirate. And forget with me."

"Forget what?" he muttered, smiling, as he lowered her body to the sleeping bag and covered it with his own.

It was much later that the *Spiritos* intruded into their thoughts—the swish of water against her hull, the deep vibration felt through the wall of the cabin as they leaned against it. Jake held her head against his shoulder. Her hair spilled over his chest, the long, warm-silk strands stirred by the breeze. She smelled of sea air and sun.

Images stirred in his mind, layered so deeply he couldn't distinguish them—sky this blue, arching over a sea that was alive, moving with a rhythm of swell and tide and wind that freed anyone who paid attention to it from all the troubles he'd tangled himself up in.

He stroked her hair. "Sweet."

He didn't know he'd spoken aloud until she murmured, "What is?"

He laughed, taken aback. "I was thinking about being kidnapped. It's not bad."

"I had to do it. I missed the sea. I knew it would be a day like this."

"You knew it when you planned the abduction?"

"Yes."

His hand moved again in her warm hair. "I believe you, Sea Sprite. You know this ocean. You have ocean instincts."

"So do you, Jake Marlow."

"No."

"Maybe you do. Maybe *instinct*'s just another word for knowing all the clues. Like when you sometimes look at all the instruments and you can't consciously remember what they say, but you have them in your subconscious and you know what they *mean*."

He chuckled with her. "Yeah. I suppose." He was silent a moment, then he said, "When I was thirteen, I figured out that you could use a depth sounder to find fish. You know, that little half ping you get when it's not really sounding on the bottom. I was convinced I could find whales with it. I practiced, plotted the readings with the next sighting. When I thought I had it down, I showed my grandfather one day when we were out on a reconnaissance run. I thought I'd impress him."

"Did you?"

He chuckled again. "I don't know. He told me before I went in for fish finding I'd better get to know how to run the boat, and he figured it was time I took charge of her myself. He strolled out on deck, wouldn't answer any of my damn questions." He let out a breath. "I was shaking in my sneakers, convinced I couldn't even remember how to steer, and I could see my grandfather stretched out in a deck chair shooting the breeze with the rest of the crew."

"I take it you didn't sink her," Maria said.

"No. I ran her all afternoon and took her into harbor. My grandfather finally came back to the wheelhouse when we came in past the breakwater, but he still didn't say anything, just watched me. I had my eyes glued to the depth sounder, scared to death I was going to run her aground outside the channel.

"But after that I knew what a depth sounder was for."

"Not for finding whales, huh?"

"My grandfather brought me up, Sea Sprite. He taught me to bring the investment home safely."

"Did you run his boats after that?"

"Yes. As soon as I could get licensed. I never thought of doing anything else. But then, I was a Marlow."

She tipped her head back against his shoulder. "I don't blame you. I would have given . . . oh, my first communion dress, for that chance, back then."

He smiled at her, gathering her hair into his hand and letting it spill out again. "I wish I'd seen you in your first communion dress. I bet you were beautiful. I would have given you all my best baseball cards. My sand-dollar collection. Every single one of my dried starfish."

Her shoulders shook. "I wouldn't have cared much

for the baseball cards. But all those starfish . . . you'd have my heart forever. I'll give it to you just for the thought."

And I'll take it, Maria Santos, just the way I took whatever chance I got from being born a Marlow. His arms tightened around her, and his eyes closed as he struggled with a wave of guilt. He had little more to give her now than dead starfish. Little more than regret and eventual hurt. But he wished, for the first time in years, that he did.

They sighted Seal's Island by mid-morning and anchored off the south cliffs, outside the sheltered cove, which wasn't navigable on the half tide.

Maria set out the hydrophones, watching Jake humor her in the preparations. Tomorrow, she thought, or the next day, he might show up with a tape of Aretha Franklin or Bruce Springsteen and try to con her into believing he'd recorded "whale songs" when he was out. He used humor to keep himself distant from the things he didn't trust.

Joaquim found them two hours after they'd anchored, and, as if he knew the power of surprise, astonished them with a rush of sound through the underwater microphone before he breached fifty yards from the boat.

Jake's leashed excitement translated itself to Maria through his hands, clenching tightly enough on her shoulders to make her wince. But she laughed, too, eager and delighted with his reaction. His deep, chuckling, "Damn!" was more welcome than any scholarly treatise on cetaceans. She knew what he would say next.

"How'd he know we were here?"

"Heard it through the grapevine, I imagine."

His arms tightened around her shoulders, covered by the light shirt she'd put on when the sun got high. "He doesn't do that for everyone, you know. The other boats seldom see Joaquim."

"He likes this spot. Who else comes here?"

"I don't know." She felt him turn his head toward the islands. "Someone, though. Since the last rain. There are footprints on our beach."

She followed his glance. "*Our* beach?"

"Our beach," he repeated emphatically. "Our whale. Our ocean."

"Sounds like kind of a romantic notion, for a Marlow."

He met her eyes, then shook his head. "I was thinking of a small condo development, a couple of subdivisions, prime real estate."

She smiled, still full of elation from the whale sighting. "No, you weren't."

"No," he agreed. "I wasn't. I was thinking of buried treasure."

"What kind of buried treasure?" she asked him, knowing the answer.

"Come back here to the sleeping bag. I'll show you."

It was pirate's treasure they shared, and Maria savored it as such: found gold, unexpected, not intended for the owners who shared it now, destined to slip through their fingers with a change of luck. Pirate's gold didn't hold much future. You couldn't ask that of it. And you could enjoy it only if you suspended expectations and put your trust in dreams.

Jake managed it for most of the afternoon. As the sun lowered across the water and she lay in his arms watching it, he murmured her name, and she felt a vague premonition in the tightening of his arm. "I wish we could stay here forever," he said.

She didn't answer him, but her hand moved up to clasp his.

"Hell," he went on, "why not? We could do it. We could raid other whale-watching boats for food and water. And sleeping bags, if we wear out this one."

She released a small sound that wasn't quite a laugh.

He let the silence stretch out. "There's the fleet to get back to, Sea Sprite."

She nodded.

"Maria . . . I want to say . . ."

Protest sluiced through her. *No. Don't say it.* But she didn't speak the words.

"Maybe these problems with the fleet will be just some minor . . ."

"Maybe," she said finally.

She could feel him trying to calculate the price of their stolen pirate's gold, trying to figure out some way to pay her share with his guilt. "But what if they're not, Maria?" he said at last. "What if you've . . . trusted the wrong person?"

She sat up and pushed herself around to face him. "Then I've trusted the wrong person."

"I don't want you to get hurt." There was an edge of anger in his voice, the frustration of not being entirely in control.

"I know," she said softly. She stood up and moved to take in the hydrophone. He was frowning at her when she turned back to the wheelhouse. "You can't know the future, Jake," she told him. "Whatever it is, we'll deal with it when it comes."

His face kept the black scowl for a moment, then she

saw his shoulders relax with reluctant acceptance of what she was saying.

"Come on," she said. "Let's head back."

His acceptance lasted for half the distance back to harbor.

Then their pirate's luck ran out.

Nine

Standing in the wheelhouse, his mind on Maria, Jake didn't register the first cough of the engine. When it sputtered again, he saw Maria frown and glance at the fuel gauge.

The engine skipped once more, giving the *Spiritos* a little lurch as it cut back in.

Apprehension needled into him, then, sharp as a cutting knife, the thought that they'd been sabotaged. He sucked in a bite of air. Maria's head turned. "I'll go below," he snapped, ignoring her surprised, wide-eyed reaction. "Don't leave the throttle."

He was halfway down when the starboard engine snarled to silence, and *Spiritos* settled in the water as she slowed. Jake took the last two steps to the engine room and yanked open the door.

A cloud of black smoke and the smell of diesel fuel filled the space around the starboard engine. The fuel line clicked as Maria jiggled the throttle, trying to kick in the engine, but it didn't so much as sigh. He knew without even looking at it that they'd lost it.

"What is it?" Maria called down to him.

Jake's gaze ran over the engine. There were a dozen ways an engine could fail by accident, but only a few logical ones if someone wanted to do it. Water in the fuel tank was the easiest.

"I'm going to pull one of the filters," he yelled back.

There was silence from above. He didn't have to tell her what he suspected. She was too good a navigator not to figure it out on her own.

She didn't ask him until he'd pulled the filter and gone back up, his face set in anger. "Water," he ground out. "In the fuel. Quite a bit. If we're lucky, it won't foul the other engine, and we'll make it home."

She nodded, silent, then reached for the radio, ignoring everything but the practical facts of their situation. An answering voice squawked back. "We've lost power on one engine," she told the harbor station. "We're headed in on the other." The voice asked for a position. She gave it, repeated that they were okay, and signed off.

When she reached toward the CB, Jake put his hand over hers. "No need to announce it to anyone who didn't already hear," he said. "Time enough to tell my grandfather when we get back."

He watched as the full comprehension that they'd been sabotaged came into her face. *Spiritos* chugged up the side of a swell sluggishly, on half power, then slid over the top with a shimmy to starboard, fighting her one-engined push to stay on course.

Maria let out a long breath, then touched his arm lightly, accepting the facts without comment.

She was right, he thought. No comment in the world would change their predicament. But the picture in his mind of Maria as she could have been, alone, caught in a storm, clawed at his emotions. Self-blame fueled the rage he felt rising in his gut. He'd spent the day making love to her when he should have been tracking down whoever would put her in danger. He'd accused her of being too trusting, but he himself had been blind and self-absorbed and not too far this side of stupid.

He didn't realize she was staring at him until he opened his eyes.

Her chest rose and fell once, then she said, "You take the throttle. I'll keep track of our position."

He moved up to the wheel, glad to be doing something besides chewing on his anger. The *Spiritos* pitched over another swell, and he muttered a sharp epithet.

"Are you swearing at my boat, Captain?" she asked him a little wryly.

"No. At myself."

Her smile flashed. "Practicing, so you'll be good at it?"

"I'm already good at it."

"I figured you were," she said. "Being a Marlow."

He glanced at her, silent.

She hadn't heard anything compared to the blue streak that was running through his head.

The Marlow dock was deserted when they limped into harbor and secured the boat beside Maria's dory. She glanced toward the house with apprehension. A single light burned in Wyatt's study.

Jake had said almost nothing on the run into the harbor, but she'd felt his tension building, instead of dissipating, as they came closer to home.

Wyatt would have to be told of the danger to his fleet. There was bound to be an explosion between the two Marlow men, who couldn't express their feelings for each other except in anger.

And she was smack in the middle of it now, caught between the man who trusted her with his fleet and the one she'd entrusted with her body . . . and her heart.

When she stepped onto the catwalk, she was shaking. "Come on," Jake said, circling her shoulders. "You're cold. Come up to the house and I'll get you a drink."

"I don't think you can. Mrs. Salintes doesn't keep the liquor cabinet stocked."

"I have a bottle in my room."

She gave a short laugh. "Like sneaking it in the college dorm?"

Still, the thought of a drink was welcome. She let him walk her to the house's back entrance and along the hallway to his room. He closed the door behind him, flicked on the portable heater, and fished under the bed for his stashed bottle and two glasses.

Half smiling at their college-dorm transgression, she looked around his room, at the bookcases, high school trophies, the old spyglass up-ended on a corner table, while he poured the Scotch. The heater whirred into the silence as he handed her a glass.

Before she could raise it to her lips, his hands cupped her face and his mouth came down on hers, hard, claiming her in a kiss that shook her with the force of its urgency. Her drink wavered in her hand, unnoticed. She might have let it drop to the floor, but at that moment the door burst open, and Wyatt stepped into the room.

She jumped back from Jake as if they'd been caught necking in the dorm parlor. Wyatt's gaze narrowed on her, taking in the speakeasy drink, the rise of color in her face, her discomposure, her just-kissed mouth, then the fierce blue eyes flicked toward his grandson. "Is this what you came here for?" he demanded.

The hardness in Jake's eyes almost made Maria flinch. "Come in, Wyatt," he said sarcastically.

"I didn't expect that I should have to knock," Wyatt said.

"I didn't expect I'd have to lock the door," Jake countered.

"You wouldn't have to, if your intentions were *honorable*."

Jake's hand tightened around his glass. "What the hell is that supposed to mean?"

"I hired her," Wyatt said, gesturing to Maria. "I brought her here, and I'm not going to see her come to any harm in my house!"

"Wyatt—" Maria began.

"I don't want to see her come to any harm either," Jake said. "Not in your house, not on one of your boats, not while she's working for your fleet!"

Wyatt glared at his grandson. "What're you talking about?"

"The *Spiritos* barely made it back to harbor tonight. There's water in the fuel tanks. Enough to choke off one engine and threaten the other. How do you suppose that much water got there?"

"Are you sayin' someone put it there?"

"Yes."

"Now, you listen to me, young—"

"No. You listen," Jake interrupted. "This is the fifth 'accident' in two months—and this one could've put one of your employees in danger. I think the fleet's being sabotaged, and I think it's time to call in the police."

There was a sharp silence in the room, marked by Maria's indrawn breath, then Wyatt raised his hand, index finger pointing accusingly. "Is that what you've been doin' here? Sneakin' around my house and my business 'cause you think I can't keep tabs on it myself?"

"Wyatt," Maria said. "In another month you *will* be keeping tabs on it yourself. You've built Marlow's into a very profitable business. That's why it might be vulnerable."

"You agree with him, then? He's been whispering sweet nothings in your ear and sneaking you up to his room?"

"There hasn't been any *sneaking*, Wyatt."

"No?" He rounded on Jake. "How long have you been sneakin' around investigating *sabotage*?"

"Since I got here," Jake said through clenched teeth.

"Did you know about that?" Wyatt demanded of Maria.

She stared back at him, gathering her thoughts. *Let me say the right thing,* she thought, but she never got the chance.

"Yes, she knew about it," Jake said, as if he had every right to speak for her without asking her opinion. "She had a right to know about it, dammit! Last night the *Dolphin* rammed her boat because someone untied the lines. Today the *Spiritos* could've been stranded out on the Bank, at the mercy of some criminal you don't want to acknowledge." His voice was hard, accusing, as cynical as his grandfather's could be. "It's time to stop it, Wyatt."

"Is that so?" Wyatt spat.

"Wyatt—" Maria said urgently.

"Yes! That's so."

"You think I put Maria in danger? You think that's the way I treat my employees?"

Maria started to step between them, her eyes flicking from one to the other, but it was too late, she realized. For all intents and purposes she might as well not be there, except as a prize for them to fight over. They were as locked in battle as two rival warriors on a field as old as time.

"All right, then!" Wyatt thundered. "You're both fired! I don't put my employees in danger, and I don't need anyone sneaking around in my house and my business tellin' me that's what I'm doing!" His chin jutted out fiercely, and his gaze locked with his grandson's. "I don't need you! I don't need your investment money and I don't need your undercover investigations. You can take the *Dolphin* for your thirty percent and get out!"

He swung toward Maria. "And you get the *Spiritos* over to the boatyard and get 'er fixed. Tell them to send me the bill."

"Do you think that's going to end it?" Jake demanded.

Wyatt ignored him. "If I see either one of those boats at my dock come morning, I'll call the harbormaster and have 'em towed away."

He spun on his heel and stalked out of the room without looking back. The door banged shut behind him so hard, it shook.

Too stunned for anything but automatic reaction, Maria moved to the door, her worry for Wyatt pushing all other thoughts aside. The older man was halfway down the hall, with Mrs. Salintes hurrying toward him. Maria stopped. The housekeeper would be a better calming influence on Wyatt than she would.

Or Jake.

A shaft of anger tightened her fingers on the door. She spun back to Jake, her face taut.

He stared at her, his gaze narrowed and angry for a moment, then the breath went out of him, and his shoulders dropped. "I'm sorry," he said brusquely. "I shouldn't have gotten you involved in this."

"No. You shouldn't."

"If there was any way I could have—"

"You could have let me speak for myself to your grandfather. I've been doing it for two months now. I know how."

"You think he was going to listen to reason?"

"I don't know. I didn't hear much *reason* being spoken here tonight."

"I was telling him the *truth,* dammit! I'm sorry about the way I did it. Maybe I shouldn't have brought you into it, but I didn't have much choice. He wouldn't face the facts any other way."

"The facts?" She shook her head. "No. What he can't face is the way they make him feel. And neither can you. You hide behind business concerns and safety issues and what happened to *my* boat. And you used *me,* Jake Marlow, to get to your grandfather."

"I used what I had to, dammit. You were on that boat. Don't you realize what could have happened to you out there? It's in your interest to have this out in the open."

"I don't need to have you tell your grandfather what *my* interest is," she said, her voice low and furious. "Tell him what *your* interest is, Jake Marlow. If you care so much what happens to this business, tell him that straight out. If you want to come back to work in it, tell him that too."

Jake's eyes, fierce with intent, so much like his grandfather's, returned the challenge in her gaze as ruthlessly as any pirate who had ever roamed the seas, taking what he wanted, sailing away from what he wanted to leave. Her heart hung between them—her own feelings, stated and open.

She watched the angry passion in his face war with the stark, cynical control he'd been schooled to, and had schooled himself to. For a brief, charged moment she saw something in his eyes—some emotion—that made her heart stop, but then he raked his hand viciously through his hair. "I never said I wanted to come back, Maria. You knew that, dammit! I stopped chasing whales a long time ago. I never said I wanted to go back."

"No." She lifted her chin. "But I never thought you'd keep me from doing it."

He muttered a crude epithet and took a step toward her. She thought for a moment he would reach for her, but he jammed his hands into his pockets and stayed where he was, bringing himself under control by visible effort. "I wasn't trying to get you fired, dammit."

She kept silent, listening to her heartbeat.

"Look—it's not the only job in Gull Cove. You don't need my grandfather. You don't need this job. You could make more money working as a consultant for marine insurance."

She stared at him, trying to connect with what he was saying. "I don't want to be a consultant in marine insurance, Jake."

"So don't do that. Work on the water. I've got a hundred-and-ten-foot boat. You can run it."

"The *Dolphin*?"

"Yes."

She drew in a sharp breath that seared all the way down to her lungs and laid bare in one painful instant the hurt that was beneath her anger. Unconsciously she reached a hand toward the shelf beside her for support. Her fingers closed on the brass spyglass and she clutched it as if it were a lifeline. Jake Marlow, the man who had taken her heart, her body, her trust, had offered her back something as cynical and mercenary as a sack of money.

Her voice shook when she spoke. "The *Dolphin* already has a captain. What about Miguel?"

He didn't have an answer, as she'd known he wouldn't. His mouth twisted, then he pulled his hands out of his pockets. "Maria—"

"No." She backed away from him. "No. I'm not the woman you want to hire, Jake Marlow. I don't think you can afford me."

She left him there, pushing out the door and making her way down the hall by instinct more than by sight.

Her eyes were blurred and wet, and there was a tight band around her chest that threatened to choke the breath out of her lungs if she didn't make it outside, to the docks, to the salt air of the ocean.

She realized, when she reached the beach, that she was still clutching Jake's spyglass. She stuffed it into her pocket, hunched her shoulders, and put one foot blindly in front of the other, following the line of surf down the harbor beach toward the point. The tide was low, the wind whipping the harbor waves into ragged edges.

Maria forced herself to notice the essential patterns of wind and tide, the shorebirds disturbed from their night roost, the shift of the sand under her feet. She needed to notice them. She needed the sounds and the smells to keep her from falling into a world where she couldn't trust herself, where her feelings, her judgment, her heart could so easily betray her.

She clutched the spyglass in her pocket with fist-clenching strength, which kept the pain from tearing through her before she could handle it. Stopping at the edge of the deserted town beach, staring out toward the harbor, she ignored the tears making wet tracks on her cheeks and forced herself to note that the wind was southeast, moderately brisk, that it would be opposed to the direction the sea was running outside the harbor. She could imagine how it would feel to be out there, pulled in two directions, fighting the current and the wind, cursing the bad luck or bad judgment or foolish impulse that had brought you there, that had made you think you could handle it.

She twisted her fingers around the spyglass. He'd warned her. He'd tried to tell her not to trust him. And she'd convinced herself she knew, she could risk it, she could make love to him and take whatever time they had together, then let the rest go. She'd convinced herself that anger and hurt were a price she was willing to pay.

But she hadn't counted on this bleak, vast loneliness that filled the cove and the harbor and spilled out beyond the point into the whole North Atlantic.

The lights of a fishing boat appeared beyond the breakwater at the far end of the town beach. Maria watched it absently. It was the Pereira boat. Miguel's fiancée's family. Lucy Pereira worried when her father went out in bad weather, Miguel said. Her father was so ambitious, so driven. He'd go out in anything if he thought the trip would bring money.

Maria hunched her shoulders as a shiver traveled up her spine. She pulled her gaze away from the boat and stared down at her feet as she walked toward the breakwater, moving with more purpose, cold now, but still unready to go back.

The Pereira slip at the pier was empty, offering no clue as to why the boat was gone.

At the end of the dock, though, taking two spaces, the caterer's truck was parked, dark and obviously left for the night. Frowning, Maria stared at it, picturing it, for no reason she could account for, parked at the Marlow dock in front of the *Dolphin.*

A moment later she heard the distant but unmistakable sound of a small outboard motor starting up, revving, then settling into a thin, steady drone. She stared out at the dark water, locating it by sound, searching for the running lights.

There were no lights.

She turned her head sharply back toward the pier, scanning the slips. The Pereira's skiff was missing. They could have taken it on board, but usually, even if the boat was out, the skiff was pulled up on shore.

Her heart started to pound. The boat. The caterer's truck. The skiff.

The spyglass was still in her pocket. She pulled it out, held it to her eye, and adjusted it. The water was dark, the spyglass awkward and unfamiliar, but there was just enough light reflected from the harbor for her to see something that shouldn't be out there . . . just enough magnification to identify it.

Jake.

Adrenaline slammed a fist into her midsection. She knew what had happened, as if she'd seen the whole thing. The caterer's truck had been outside the house when she left. Jake must have seen it, followed it, watched the Pereira boat go out, and taken the skiff, rowing out beyond earshot before he started the engine.

She was running before she consciously knew what she planned to do, heading back along the beach and cursing the sand that dragged at her feet and slowed her down.

The *Spiritos* was low in the water when she swung

on board, panting. She pulled open the door to the instrument room and flicked on the radar.

She couldn't find him. A flash of pure panic shot through her, then she caught a tiny, irregular flick on the scanning screen that must have been Jake.

In a wooden boat, with a growing swell, he was hard to pick up. Outside the harbor no one who wasn't already alerted to him would read him. But the Pereira boat was easy to spot, already beyond the point and headed out to sea. On a straight course toward Seal's Island, ten miles out.

She shut off the radar, her hand shaking, and closed her eyes, offering up a swift prayer.

Ambivalence, conflicting feelings, anger were all washed out of her like so much flotsam. She felt only the pure, worried fear of a woman whose man was out to sea in a boat that might not bring him back.

She clutched at the spyglass as if it were a talisman. She didn't dare take the *Spiritos* out. And at any rate, there was no way she could follow anyone without being picked up on radar. But she had her dory, a small, high-sided boat, a compass, and a full tank of gas. She could make better speed than the fishing boat, even on an indirect course. As long as she'd guessed their destination right . . .

She shut off the fear in her mind and started gathering together all the things she needed.

Ten

Jake edged the skiff up over the top of the next wave and pitched into the trough. The bow slapped down into it and sent a sheet of drenching spray back toward the stern. He didn't bother to swear. He was already soaked, already too familiar with the awkward pitch of the small boat in this sea.

In some perverse way he welcomed the fight. It gave him a direction for his anger and something to do besides standing in his grandfather's hallway picturing Maria walking away from him.

You can't afford me.

He tightened his grip on the outboard handle and fixed his gaze on the distant lights of the Pereira boat. He'd come close to grabbing her, hauling her against him, forcing her to acknowledge what she'd given him—her laughter, her sweet, responsive body, her trust. But he wasn't quite the son of a bitch it would take to do that, despite the overwhelming force of his need for her. He'd never used force on a woman in his life, never before been tempted to.

Of course not, a cynical voice in the back of his mind taunted. *You just bought them.*

With a sharp yank of his arm Jake nosed the skiff into the next swell, bracing himself for the next slap of

cold salt water. It hit him like his own shortcomings—
cold, relentless, and backed by more of the same.

He'd given up counting the ways he didn't like himself. He found himself, instead, counting the things
he didn't have to blame himself for. That list was
a lot shorter. He'd gotten through to Wyatt—probably—and he'd left *Spiritos* safe in her slip, at least
until Wyatt called the harbormaster on her. Jake was
pretty sure there wouldn't be any mischief done that
night. If his guess was close, the mischief makers
were all otherwise occupied. And at least—God, he
gave thanks for that—Maria wasn't out in this. He
wondered if she'd be with him in this skiff if they
hadn't argued, then he shut the thought off with a
sharp, muttered curse. The memory of her loyalty,
her courage, her trust—the trust he'd forfeited—
twisted in his gut like a knife.

Better to keep his thoughts on what he was doing.
The compass—if he could trust it—indicated he was
headed southeast, in the direction of Seal's Island. If
the Pereira boat passed the island, he'd let them go,
beach the skiff, and wait for better weather and day-
light to head back. But he had a strong suspicion the
fishing boat wouldn't go any farther than the island.
He glanced at his watch, calculating distance and
time, then stared back at the lights of the boat he
was following.

He'd lost track of time when he saw the fishing
boat's lights wink out over the black sea. For a
moment he thought he'd lost sight of them in a
swell. They didn't reappear, though, and he realized
the boat must have rounded the eastern edge of Seal's
Island, where the high cliffs cut off his view. He cut
his engine and got out the oars.

The Pereira boat, he guessed, was holding off the

southeastern shore, where deep water offered the only anchorage for a boat that size. If they were off-loading from the beach where he and Maria had seen footprints that day, they'd be using a small power boat. Three minutes later he heard the drone of their outboard. Not so small. But at least their engine was loud enough to mask the sound of his rowing.

He brought the skiff straight in to the western shore, shipping the oars as he drifted closer and testing the bottom with the anchor.

The skiff dipped awkwardly as the anchor payed out and didn't find bottom. Cursing under his breath, he glanced toward the channel, thinking of the sheltered cove where Maria anchored the *Spiritos*, but he didn't dare risk it. Even from where he was, he could see flashlight beams flickering out over the channel from the beach.

He rowed closer to the cliffs, tried the anchor again. It bottomed. Barely. But he wasn't going to get better anchorage. He'd have to trust it.

He shipped the oars and slid over the side of the skiff, gritting his teeth against the cold water.

Just one good look. One good view of what they were doing. He couldn't hope to stop them. But he could get enough information to nail them when he called the coast guard.

The noisy, overpowered speedboat they were using was in his favor. When it buzzed the beach, Jake pulled himself out of the water onto an overhanging rock. His first surge of elation coursed through him. Another six inches and he'd be over the top. Golden. Mission accomplished.

But he hadn't counted on the wake from the speed-boat. Behind him, the wash of the wave surged out of the channel and along the shore of the island. He heard a scrape, the complaining squeak of a painter rubbing on an old gunwale, then the slap of waves against wood. Turning his head, he watched his skiff float into the channel and head toward the beach, straight into the speedboat's bowlight.

Maria heard the shouts as the drone of the speedboat cut out. Lights flickered erratically across the channel, reflecting glints of yellow against the cliff walls of the cove where she was anchored on the opposite side of the channel from the small beach. Sculling with one oar, she brought the dory closer to the channel and strained her ears to listen.

A boat. They were shouting about a loose skiff, pulled away from its anchor. *Jake's.*

"That's ours," a deep voice called out. She recognized Lucy Pereira's father Tome, sounding surprised and angry. "What the hell is it doing here?"

Then another voice: "Did it come off the boat?"

Jake must not be in it. Dear God, why not?

There were all too many reasons why not. He'd gone over, capsized in the surf, never made it to the island. . . .

She tasted a rush of adrenaline, metallic and terrifying, and tried to imagine a way Jake would come safe through this.

The tug on the dory's stern shocked her so much, she nearly cried out, whirling around, clutching the oar.

Two hands grabbed the stern of the dory, pulled, and Jake's face appeared above the gunwale. "Dammit, Maria," he mumbled, his voice low and irate. "What the hell are you doing here?"

Her legs sagged beneath her in relief, and she sat down hard on the bow seat. Jake used her counterweight to pull himself over the stern, and she moved toward him without thinking, throwing her arms around his shoulders, holding him with all her strength. "I heard you go out," she whispered. "I was on the beach. I saw the fishing boat, and then the caterer's truck. When you started the outboard, I noticed their skiff was gone. I tracked the big boat on radar. Oh, Jake—" Her breath came out on a near sob, and she swallowed it back, conscious of the shouting voices beyond the overhang of the cliff.

The snarl of the speedboat's engine drowned the voices beyond the cove. She felt Jake's body tense, then he put her away from him, reached for an oar, and silently stroked the dory in under the cliff's overhang.

"Stay still," he whispered as the drone of the engine increased. "They won't be looking for a dory. They've found the skiff. They'll be looking for me on the beach."

The boat buzzed past the cove, flicking a flashlight over the calm water. Maria's throat tightened with the sure conviction that they would be seen, but the light moved on to the shore where the skiff had been anchored.

The speedboat slowed to an idle, letting them hear the cadence of rising voices.

"They're still arguing over whether the skiff was on the boat," Maria murmured.

"It won't take them long to figure it out. They're keyed up, but they're not stupid."

"What are they doing here?" she whispered.

"I don't know. I didn't get a chance to see it. Drugs, I'd bet. This must have been the drop-off point. Pereira

will pick up the cargo, take it in to some fishing por
drop it off in a load of lobsters."

The speedboat buzzed back along the channe
whining like an electric saw, then slowed an
approached the beach. Hurried, nervous voice
argued about loading the last of the cargo.

"I've got to get a look at what they're loading,
Jake said.

She stared at him, her eyes widening, then sh
shook her head. "No. Let them go. We can call th
coast guard when they're gone."

"And let Pereira hear the message? They'll be lis
tening for that. If they get out of here clean, there'
be no way to stop them. They'll transfer the carg
again, and no one the wiser. I have to see wha
it is."

"Let it go, Jake," she said, her voice tense.

"No. This has something to do with the fleet. I'r
going to find out what."

He let go of her and slipped over the side befor
she could stop him. She clutched the gunwale o
her dory and watched him, swimming with strong
silent strokes out of the cove.

She sucked in a lungful of air, realizing she wa
holding her breath to hear what was happening
Voices. Splashing. The clunk of wood against woo
and an impatient reprimand. Some comment abou
the skiff, edged with threat. They'd be looking fo
Jake, scanning the beach, the rocks. . . .

Just let them finish their business and leave.

"What the hell was that?" someone shouted. "Cu
that engine!" The speedboat went silent, and Maria'
heart slammed into her throat.

"Who's out there?"

Maria leaned over the bow of the dory, starin

around the rock cliff. On the opposite shore a circle of ripples fanned out from behind a rock. Jake, slipping into the water. *Don't notice. Don't see it.*

"It's nothing," a sharp voice called. "There's nothing there."

"Fool!" Tome Pereira yelled. "Who came out in that skiff? He's here somewhere."

There was an angry splash, then Tome's shout. "Show yourself!" His flashlight scanned the shore. "Don't be stupid. I know you're not the law."

Behind him, there was nervous muttering.

"Who are you?" Another silence, then, "Jake Marlow?"

All her senses screamed a silent protest, but Tome went on. "Is that who you are? Not the old man, that's for sure."

Tome was guessing, she realized. Guessing close.

"Let's make a deal," the man shouted. "Show yourself, come out with us. I'll cut you in."

Silence. Maria stared toward the ripples. They'd all but dissipated.

"I'll make it even better," Tome offered. "When I get your grandfather's fleet, I'll cut you in on that too. A better deal than you have with him. Forty percent."

Tome's light swung, indicating a direction. Telling one of his men where to search. Had Jake seen it? Her fingers gripped the side of her dory in fear.

The voice thundered through the unnatural silence, deep and compelling, mesmerizing. "You don't have much choice here, Jake Marlow. Show yourself. If we have to find you, it won't go well. And we will find you. We can leave you here, come back when it's light. Where will you hide then, my friend? You have no radio, no signal. Don't be foolish. Show that you'll do business with us."

Tome's voice had moved, coming closer to Jake's hiding place. He was searching the shore.

Straining her eyes toward the rock where she'd seen the ripples, Maria made out a movement. Jake was swimming away from the shore, across the channel, keeping the rocky cliff between himself and the beach.

She shipped the oars, muting the sound with her hands. If he could make it to the cove, they might slip out around the south end of the island, get far enough away from there to foil the search. . . .

"I'm waiting, my friend. But I'm not a patient man."

Dear God, she prayed. Just the two words. She could see him now, halfway across the channel, swimming diagonally toward the cove. *Just another twenty yards. Don't see him.*

Tome's flashlight skimmed across the channel, and there was a sudden shout.

Maria made a squeaky, panicked sound, then stopped breathing.

"There he is! Get him!"

Jake dove, leaving a wake of turbulence. The speedboat hissed, then whined like an attack dog, circling around toward Jake, its headlight a swathe of deadly illumination.

Maria threw herself into the rowing thwart, pulling hard on the oars, desperate to get closer to Jake.

Senses tuned to him, she heard the creak of her oars, the revving of the speedboat bearing down on him, then, beneath the closer sounds, an irregular rushing wake.

The identification came at once: It was a whale swimming near the surface, but unnaturally, oddly, with a kind of desperation she could feel rather than hear.

She pulled again on the oars, just clearing the cove, her eyes, her muscles, straining toward Jake. He was swimming hard, trying to reach the lee shore to escape the boat, but too far, too slow, caught and thrown back by a pressure wave rushing up the channel.

Maria stared as a whale roared into the channel, plowing up the water like a skier, dragging a wake of turbulence a hundred yards long.

The speedboat whined into high pitch, turning, as the great whale scored the water between Jake and the deadly speedboat. The boat's engine gurgled and died, and the air was filled with shouts and confusion.

"The prop's fouled! Fishing seine!"

Someone cursed. She heard the creak and swish of a boat being hauled backward, then a howl of fear. "The whale was dragging a fishing seine! It's fouled the prop!"

"Cut it loose!" Tome shouted from shore. "Do it, you coward!"

The boat slammed into the rock cliff. Wood splintered, creaked, and a cry of relief shouted over the channel. The speedboat's engine started again.

Jake surfaced inside the cove, ten feet from her dory, and got his hand on an oar. Maria pulled him in toward the dory. He gripped the gunwale and held on, panting.

From across the channel Tome was barking orders to the panicked speedboat driver, organizing the crew on the beach to get them away. Offshore, in the direction of the anchored fishing boat, the panicked, irregular thrashing of the whale rose over the rhythm of the surf. The speedboat engine droned as the boat, riding lower in the water, moved off.

Slowly, moving hand over hand toward the stern, Jake let himself believe he would get out of this alive.

Maybe.

He hefted himself over the dory's stern, taking the hand Maria held out to him. He pulled her against him, wrapping his arms around her, cradling her head against him with the strength of desperation.

"It was Joaquim," she said against his shoulder.

"I know." He held her tighter, dripping cold water into the dory.

She said nothing, but a low, strangled sound caught in her throat.

Jake cupped her head, stroking her back. "It's all right. They'll leave. And they think I've got no way out of here. They want to get away from that whale."

She was trembling, her teeth chattering as much as his were. She was breathing in quick gulps, holding her breath in between to listen to the speedboat, the distant voices, the irregular thrashing offshore.

The dory had drifted toward the channel. Jake reached for one of the oars and pushed against the cliff to get them back farther into the cove.

Maria's glance was a silent question.

"They won't see us," he whispered. He pulled her against him again. "You should have stayed where you were, Sea Sprite. You couldn't outrun that speedboat."

"I would have radioed, identified them. They might have been more inclined to leave us alone then."

He gave a quiet bark of laughter that held as much resignation as humor. She'd had a better plan than he had. He should have known.

"Did you see what you wanted?" she asked.

"Yeah. Crates of coffee creamer, stacked up in the boat."

"Coffee creamer?"

He nodded, his chin digging into her shoulder. "It's the kind you've seen before. There are three of them right now stacked in the *Dolphin*'s galley."

"*Three* crates of coffee creamer? But why—" Her voice broke off. "Oh," she said, almost inaudibly. She pulled away from him. "You still think Miguel is part of this."

He hesitated. "I don't know. Maybe he was delivering. Maybe he doesn't know about it. Maybe the stuff was planted there, to get the fleet into trouble. Miguel doesn't run the galley. If one of the mates opens that box and finds something funny in it, a small amount, maybe, there's no way everyone won't know it. What kind of business you think the fleet will do if the word gets around it was involved with drugs? Even if everyone's found innocent, the business will be hurt."

She studied him. He could almost feel her quick intelligence spinning out the possibilities—what he'd told her, what they'd witnessed. "Will Wyatt have called the harbormaster already to have the *Dolphin* towed?"

"I don't know. If he did, it's going to sound pretty funny to the harbormaster. I doubt he'll tow her at daybreak, but I wouldn't put it past him to call the police, board her maybe, have a look around."

She let out a long breath, then glanced toward the east shore, where the rumble of a big engine was added to the confused sounds.

"They're leaving," Jake said. "They want to get away from that whale before he fouls any more propellers."

She nodded. "Joaquim." Her voice shook. Jake put

his hand over hers, and she gripped it. They sat in silence, listening to the big boat rumble away. The sound of Joaquim fighting the seine net grew more obvious.

"They're headed south, sounds like," Jake murmured.

She glanced toward her radio, and Jake followed the thought. They couldn't call a message to anyone. Tome Pereira could stash the evidence before they were caught, and the speedboat could be back to Seal's Island in minutes. He could imagine the scene too clearly: an interception, a small, arranged "accident" for Maria's dory, all too probable for an eighteen-foot boat ten miles out. They'd already been willing to risk her life on the *Spiritos*. A wave of anger welled in his chest.

"Come on," he said, letting go of her hand. "Let's get out of here."

She didn't move.

His hand on the outboard, Jake glanced toward her. "We can read them on radar, keep the island between us and them until we've got enough distance between us to head for shore."

She was so still, she might have been part of the boat, her face a pale oval in the dark, turned toward him. He frowned, feeling a ripple of uneasiness.

"What about Joaquim?" she said finally.

What about Miguel? The echo of her earlier question broke around them like phosphorescence on a dark sea. It wasn't the same question, but she was retreating from him the same way, and he felt the same premonition, the same weight of choice, the same swift, spiraling distance between them. "Maria—all we can do is call the coast guard. They'll get a team out here in the morning."

"In the morning," she repeated, toneless.

"We can't do anything else. We've got to get out of here. And even if we stayed, what could we do for Joaquim in an eighteen-foot dory, no equipment, no diving gear. . . ."

Her throat worked. He couldn't see her expression, but something in the way her eyes didn't leave his face cut into him. "What do you think we can possibly do?" he asked. His own voice had an edge of desperation.

"Probably nothing," she said at last. "And it's dangerous to try. I know. Not a good risk." Her voice was flat, resigned, too profoundly disappointed to show any emotion.

Disappointed in him, Jake thought, feeling a shaft of pain so real, it could have been the prop of a speedboat cutting him to ribbons.

It hadn't occurred to Maria to doubt that they could do it. He realized she'd been thinking they'd find a way to save her whale, turning it over in her mind, clinging to her natural trust, faith . . . and he'd crushed that faith.

Dammit, he didn't have any choice! But the wish that he did ran through him like hot steel. He gritted his teeth against the pain of it and yanked the outboard's starter cord hard enough to do damage. The engine roared to life.

Maria's knuckles went white where she gripped the stern, then she let it go, moved to the rowing thwart, and shipped the oars.

"Maria." Jake idled the engine. "He'll be all right until morning."

He almost missed the shake of her head. "No," she said softly. "He won't."

Jake stopped himself from uttering a string of

expletives he hadn't used in years. He couldn't doubt
Maria's prediction about the whale. Even if he hadn't
witnessed her instincts in that area, he knew the dan-
gers of a seine net to a creature fighting it. A creature
that had to surface to breathe every few minutes.

But she'd agreed with him. She had. They couldn't
help Joaquim. Even getting close to the whale risked
their lives. Anything caught in the net with Joaquim
would be towed, dragged under. . . .

She'd pulled herself to the center of the rowing
thwart, not looking at him, her shoulders hunched
defensively, her head bowed.

He didn't see a sheen of tears on her face, but his
own eyes burned, his own gut twisted with guilt and
despair and protest at what he had to do, what was
practical, logical. He couldn't risk it, dammit. He
couldn't risk her life, both their lives, her boat, his
grandfather's fleet.

No. So destroy her faith instead.

Blackness as menacing and impenetrable as the
cliffs looming over them seemed to seep into his
soul as he clenched his jaw and set his mind to
what they had to do: run the dory south, make it
to shore before morning, alert the coast guard. Then
settle up with his grandfather and go back to Boston.
To his steady profits, calculated risks, land-bound
ways. Without her.

Despair sucked the breath out of his lungs. That
wasn't life, he thought. His cynical, low-risk, no-faith
version of living wasn't life. Maria's faith had drawn
him to her like a beacon, a light to a foundering boat
on a black ocean. He'd needed her light, her faith,
her trust, the way he needed harbor.

And he wouldn't quench it now.

Abruptly he cut the outboard. When she looked at

him, he said, "I'll row. We'll go through the channel to him. We can't risk the prop. And maybe with no engine sound he'll slow down, let us help him."

He could have sworn he could see her eyes widen, feel her reaction of surprise and renewed hope.

"What have you got that will cut fishing seine?" he asked.

She swung around in the bow and reached for the storage locker while he took her place on the rowing thwart and pulled hard on the oars, putting all his strength into the effort.

They came into the channel, and Jake glanced over his shoulder.

"There's a good knife. It'll do," Maria said. She sat up in the bow, peering forward, then glanced back to him. "Joaquim's offshore. He's not headed for the channel."

"Okay." He kept rowing. If the whale caught them in the channel he could capsize them, catch them both up in the net. At the northeast corner the surf caught them and twisted the dory before Jake got her headed into the swell. They could hear Joaquim offshore. Jake thought the sound was less strident, slower.

Maybe the whale was weakening.

They were a hundred yards offshore when Maria turned back to him. "He's heading toward us. I think he knows we're here."

Jake felt the skin prickle on the back of his neck.

"Ship the oars," she ordered.

The immense, dark shape in the water slowed as it approached them. Then, in uncanny and unbeliev-able quiet, Joaquim pulled alongside them, dwarfing the dory, the whale's enormous bulk floating by them yard by yard, from his massive head to the pale blur of his tail. The flippers were as wide as the dory was long.

The seine net was wrapped around him, partly torn, pulled taut against the blowhole in the top of his head. Maria braced herself against the bow thwart and reached down to grasp the net before Jake could stop her. The dory jolted to a stop, then backed as the whale pulled them around, slowly, the big creature almost resting motionless in the sea.

"I'll hold us. See if you can cut the net," she said urgently.

Jake reached for the knife, leaned over, tipping precariously in the dory. He couldn't reach. Frustrated, he climbed to the stern. From there he could cut part of the net, but the tightly wrapped nylon strands that were restricting the whale's breathing were too far out of reach.

Maria glanced at him, her face taut, her body tense.

He yanked at the buttons of his shirt, peeling it off his shoulders. "I'm going in," he said. "I can't reach from here."

"Jake—"

He stopped only long enough to lock eyes with her. "Talk to him, Sea Sprite. Tell him to stay still for me. Tell him we're trying to help him."

She made a sound of protest and fear, but Jake was already over the side, into the black, cold water, sharing the sea with an immense creature who could kill him in a moment, whose intelligence and trust he was counting on.

The whale's smooth, taut, barnacle-spattered flesh bulged around the thin nylon diamonds of the net where his head had pushed partly through it. Jake grasped the trailing net, pulled himself toward Joaquim, and surfaced to gulp in air.

Joaquim was still, quiescent. To free him, Jake would have to work the knife under the net, cut outward, somehow making a big enough hole for the whale to escape.

Maria was murmuring to the whale, stroking him, calming him. Jake flicked open the knife, a six-inch curved blade meant for filleting. Wickedly sharp, it would more than likely cut the whale, or Jake, if either of them moved.

"Go easy, fella," Jake muttered. "I'm not trying to hurt you." He gulped a breath and dove. Finding the net by touch, he started to work the knife beneath the nylon. A huge shudder ripped the massive expanse of flesh, but the whale, incredibly, didn't move. The strand parted, loosening the net a few inches. Jake slid it under the next strand.

Five minutes later the net floated, loosened, around them. Jake got himself into the dory and reached down for the folds of nylon. "Row us," he told Maria. "If he stays still, we can pull it off over his head."

She got them headed away from the flippers, pulled on the oars, and the dory moved off, dragging the net with it.

"Easy, Joaquim," Jake crooned. "Just hold on a little longer. We'll do it. We'll get you free."

The net dragged at them as if trying to pull the small dory back into it, but slowly, an inch at a time, it came free. Joaquim, as if realizing he was no longer encumbered, blew once, an enormous, exultant breath, then swerved slowly away from them and swam free.

Jake didn't move for a moment, watching the dark ripple on the sea, then he felt Maria's hand on his shoulder and turned toward her. "Looks like we did it, Sea Sprite. We did it."

She nodded. The tears she hadn't shed before glistened on her eyelashes, and the soft trembling of her lips spoke of sobs held back.

They had to get away from the island, Jake thought, before Tome returned. But he stole a moment to pull her against him, wrap her in his arms, press her head against his shoulder, feel her hair on his face, his throat. He felt an ache there that could have been his own sob, until it was loosened and transformed in a deep, joy-filled laugh that echoed across the water and mingled with the surf on the island's shore.

Eleven

Morning light illuminated the hall when Jake knocked at the door of his grandfather's study. Outside, the Marlow dock baked in the sun, the tide already edging up the pilings from its low-water mark.

The door opened, and Jake faced his grandfather over the threshold. Wyatt's flinty gaze narrowed.

Jake felt the familiar rise of response, but he made himself start talking before Wyatt could begin their bickering anew. "I want to let you know what's happened," he said.

"Yes?"

"I spent the night chasing Tome Pereira out to Seal's Island. He picked up a cargo of drugs, tried to drop it off at Stirrup Rock Harbor. The Coast Guard got him this morning."

Wyatt scowled at him. "And what were you doin' mixed up in it?"

"One of his men had planted some drugs on board the *Dolphin,* trying to make trouble for us, but he confessed to it. He said Tome Pereira's been sabotaging the fleet, using the catering service to get to us."

"Tome Pereira?"

Jake nodded. "He wanted the fleet."

The older man ran a gnarled hand through his hair. "I know he did," Wyatt said, surprising him. "He's wanted it for years. Never could stand the fact that we started out equal but the whale-watching fleet makes twice as much as he does now."

Jake frowned. "You knew this?"

"No, I didn't know it!" Wyatt barked. Jake kept a determined silence, and Wyatt's glare dissipated to an irritated snort. "But I can put two and two together when you tell me he's confessed to puttin' drugs on the *Dolphin*! He tried to buy me out three months ago. I told him I wasn't interested."

"So he . . . took matters into his own hands," Jake muttered.

His grandfather nodded. "Guess he thought a little trouble would change my mind." Wyatt glowered. "Thought I was helpless now, couldn't handle it. He didn't count on the way Maria managed things—or on a nosy insurance agent." His breath hissed in through his teeth, and he glanced toward the window for a brooding moment. "Damn fool," he added, but the anger wasn't quite carried in the last words. They could almost have held a note of sympathy.

Jake kept quiet, bemused at the extent to which his grandfather had guessed the truth, and puzzled at his reaction. The older man's gaze flicked back to him. "Maria know about this?"

"She was there. At the island." He swallowed hard. "She . . . followed me."

Wyatt stared back at him, eyes shrewd. "She's in love with you?"

Jake's gaze locked with the older man's. "I don't know. All I know is that I am with her."

Wyatt was silent, then asked challengingly, "What are you going to do about it? Take her back to Boston?

Get her a job in your insurance agency? Take her away from the fleet?"

Jake felt his anger threaten to boil over. Wyatt was too close to the mark in guessing what Jake had tried to offer her, and the truth of it pinched. "*You* fired her, remember?" he said through clenched teeth. "She doesn't have a job with the fleet."

Wyatt waved a hand. "She has a job. I know damn well she's the best manager in Gull Cove. And I know damn well she doesn't belong in Boston!"

Suppressed anger burned from Jake's throat all down through his gut. He didn't let himself speak for a moment. Wyatt goaded his temper unerringly, knowing with uncanny accuracy what would get to him: Maria . . . the implication that she would be better off where she was than with Jake . . . the idea, too close to Jake's own residual fear, that he would hurt her . . . the idea, underneath all of it, that Jake should never have left Gull Cove in the first place.

Maybe he was right. Jake bit back the arguments that came so readily when Wyatt poked him with the truth. Jake had always known where he learned his cynical, hard-line view of the world from. But there was another way to look at it too. Another way to hear the truth. He'd learned it in a dark cove beside a woman who believed they could save a whale in trouble . . . and Jake had come to believe he could save himself as well.

He let out a long breath and met his grandfather's gaze without anger. "I'm not taking her back to Boston," he said levelly, offering no resistance to the barbed antagonism of his grandfather's glare. "I'm going to let her bring me home."

•   •   •

Spiritos was on a mooring offshore, riding easily on the drift of the tide. Jake watched the boat until Maria came out of the wheelhouse, her face turned toward the harbor, and crossed the deck to the stern rigging to lean out, adjusting some equipment.

The sun was hot on Jake's back, the first promise of full summer. The water was flat, a darker blue than the sky, the waves showing just a hint of white where the breakwater cut off the harbor. He stayed where he was, beside the open door of his car, until one of the yard crew glanced toward him curiously.

Jake waved at the man and slammed shut the door of his car.

He took the johnboat out to *Spiritos*, watching Maria grow closer. She leaned on the rail, relaxed, her eyes following him. She had changed to white shorts and a sleeveless, scoop-necked blouse. Her hair fanned out over her shoulder like a swathe of midnight against the bright morning.

She'd been up all night, as he had. Their vigil seemed to have slowed the pace of time between them to a tidal drift. Jake let himself on board, tied up the johnboat, then straightened, watching her again, taking her in with his senses.

"Ahoy, Captain," he said finally. "Coming aboard."

She smiled. "So I see."

Spiritos swung on her mooring. Jake was aware of water sipping at the hull, the distant sounds of the boatyard.

"Did you talk to your grandfather?"

He nodded. "You've got your job back. He wants you there tomorrow morning. Claims he never intended to fire the best manager in Gull Cove."

"The old pirate," she said. "I ought to make him give me a raise."

"I told him about Pereira. He took it pretty well. I think he knew, without admitting it, that something like that was going on."

She nodded, her smile fading. "I'm glad you did. He would have heard it sooner or later. Word's all around the boatyard already."

Jake pushed his hands into his pockets, fighting the urge to touch her. "It'll be tough on Miguel and his fiancée, won't it? I'm sorry about that."

"Yes. It will. But they'll come through it okay. Lucy Pereira comes from a strong family. She'll stand by her father, but she'll accept that he was wrong. And she has Miguel."

"Maria . . ."

When she glanced up at him, he didn't know where to start. He looked over his shoulder toward the yard. A few of the faces were turned toward them, speculative and curious about the morning's gossip.

"Can we take the *Spiritos* out?" he asked. "Before Wyatt decides he wants you to work today. I'll captain. You can catch some sleep on the way out."

"We can take her out." She smiled. "And I don't want to sleep."

"You must be dead tired, Maria."

"Are you trying to avoid talking to me, Jake Marlow?"

The corners of his mouth turned up. "No. I want to talk. I want to . . ." He let out a quick breath. "Hell, what I want to do would burn the whole yard down, Maria Santos. Maybe half the town with it. And everyone watching would sure have plenty to talk about then."

"Well, then, maybe we should get offshore a ways."

At her slow, intimate smile, Jake felt his blood heat in a visceral reaction as powerful as the tide itself.

He didn't let himself touch her as he turned toward the wheelhouse. He didn't trust himself touching her. He wanted to talk to her first, to say what he needed to say, and if he touched her once, there wouldn't be any talking.

They'd run nearly five miles out before Jake idled the engine. The *Spiritos* planed to a stop, then he killed the diesels and allowed the boat to drift.

Maria let the silence spin out around them.

She didn't know if she wanted to break it. Jake's work there was done, as of that morning. Maybe he was trying to tell her he was leaving. If he was, she couldn't stop him. She couldn't hold him, any more than Joaquim could be held in a seine net without it killing him.

She checked the gauges, marked their position on the chart, then turned off the radio. In the sudden quiet she toed off her sneakers, picked up the hydrophone, and walked out on the deck barefoot.

Jake followed her. When she turned around to face him, she saw he was carrying the spyglass she'd left in the wheelhouse the night before. He grinned at her. "What's this doing on board the *Spiritos*?"

"I walked off with it last night. I didn't realize I had it. I put it down here when I tracked you on radar going out of the harbor."

"It seems to be following me around." He set it up on end on the rail, then leaned his elbow beside it and faced out to sea. "I'm not sure why I ever kept the thing, to tell you the truth."

"It was a gift from your grandfather."

"Yeah. One Marlow pirate to another."

There was a moment of silence filled, in Maria's ears, with the sound of her own hopes, her own fears. She turned back to the rail and picked up the underwater microphone, then set it out with practiced efficiency, using the routine task to bridge the unresolved tension between them.

Jake watched her, staying just out of her way, waiting until she'd finished and turned back toward him. "Maria . . ."

She managed a slight smile. "Yes?"

"Maria." At the suddenly husky quality of his voice, a wave of response rippled through her and sent shivers chasing down her spine.

Unable to stop herself, she touched his arm.

He pulled her against him with all the fierce urgency she wanted. His breath stirred her hair, and he leaned back against the rail, taking her with him. With a glint of metal the spyglass tipped slowly, balanced for a moment on edge, then toppled off the rail.

She cried out and made a grab for it, but Jake's hand caught hers and pulled it back against his chest. The spyglass hit the water and sank, giving off a watery glimmer. "Let it go," he said.

"But—"

He laughed. "Let it go. It's time I made some new connections with my grandfather." His arms tightened around her, and she felt his laughter fade into something more serious. "I want to stay in Gull Cove. I want to work in the fleet, if I can find a way to get along with my grandfather."

"Oh, Jake," she said softly, around the lump in her throat. "I know you can."

His hand stroked the back of her head. "Will you put in a word for me?"

"Yes."

"Give me a little advice when I need it?"

"Yes."

"Keep me on track?"

"If I can."

"Marry me?"

She reared her head back to look up at his face, wondering if he'd meant it as a joke.

His voice was husky. "I've spent years proving I didn't need my grandfather's business, that I could make it on my own, just like he did. But I met you, and you gave me back something I lost. And it's something I don't want to live without, Maria." His hands framed her face, and she realized his fingers were trembling. "And I don't want to live without you."

The blunt, intense honesty unraveled her control. She covered her hands with his and let her breath sigh out on a single word.

Jake's thumb brushed across one wet track on her cheek. His lips brushed the other and followed it down to the corner of her mouth. He kissed her slowly, murmuring her name against her lips, asking her to say yes.

"Yes," she whispered.

For Jake the sibilant sound, like the sifting of water against the hull of the *Spiritos*, drew him into a world where sound was as physical as the resilience of her skin, the silk touch of her hair, the liquid heat of their joined mouths. He pulled her against him, and the crush of cotton between them whispered of desire and need. He lowered her to the sleeping bag he spread out on the deck, and the sifting rasp of nylon stoked the restless current that surged through him. He covered her breasts with his hands, and the sweet, soft sound he drew from her touched all his senses, as though her voice were kissing his skin.

She gave herself without reservation, letting her body sing for him as he thumbed open the snap of her shorts and drew them down over her hips. His hands lingered, his lips trailing sensuous heat along her stomach, the joint of her hip, her thighs. When he returned to her to kiss her breasts and suckle her nipples, his voice joined hers, murmuring praise and endearments, whispering a message incoherent except for the sound, the rhythm, the harmony.

He loved her with tenderness and passion, and with more than that: with a giving of himself that risked everything for their joining. When he merged their bodies, filling her with strength and potency, each stroke of sheathed power was a cadence of music whose harmony she knew.

He kissed her, and she felt the urgency of melodies intertwining, yearning, seeking the high, resolving note. When he climaxed, she heard the exultant, singing cry of her name, and wasn't sure she'd heard the vibrations in her ears or in her mind. It didn't matter. A moment later he took her with him into the release of that shared song.

As the echoes dissolved around them and they drifted together, they became aware of the sounds outside them: the ever-present lap of water, the breathing of the wind against wood and over water, the soft, liquid gurgle from the hydrophones.

Gradually, more by instinct than by conscious thought, Maria turned her head toward the microphone. Beneath the familiar mix of sound was a resonant throbbing almost inaudible at first. As it grew deeper and more compelling, she realized Jake was listening, too, his face still, as if all his senses were tuned to that low, intense sound.

They weren't alone. She knew it even if the sound had died with that first distant echo. Instead it swelled, echoed, reverberated through the microphone in a web of song so complex and beautiful, it filled the air around them as completely as it filled the water.

Jake held her closer, and his exultant laugh released her own delighted, amazed laughter.

"Joaquim," he said distinctly, with no question.

"Yes. Yes." She grinned at him. "Yes!"

"He's singing for you, Sea Sprite. He knows. He's doing it for you."

"He's doing it for you," she amended. "Because you saved his life."

"No. For you. Because you saved mine."

"For us, then."

He grinned again, shutting his eyes to better listen to the glorious cadence of music he thought he'd never hear.

Only when it had drifted away, the last fading echo returning to them through the fathoms of water that carried it, did Jake think to ask, "Were you recording that?"

She gazed at him, startled, then started to laugh again, for no reason she could think of. "No. I didn't have the recorder hooked up."

Jake shook his head, then smiled and touched her face, his fingers reverent. "Then we're the only ones who will ever hear that particular song, aren't we?"

"I'll hear it every time you make love to me."

"Ah, Sea Sprite." He stroked her face. "Make me hear it again."

Moments later the whale's song rose again, not in the water or the air, but in the joining of two spirits who had found their own echo of that harmony.

THE EDITOR'S CORNER

Come join the celebration next month when LOVE-
SWEPT reaches its tenth anniversary! When the line
was started, we made a very important change in the
way romance was being published. At the time, most
romance authors published under a pseudonym, but
we were so proud of our authors that we wanted to
give them the credit and personal recognition they
deserved. Since then LOVESWEPT authors have
always written under their own names and their pic-
tures appear on the inside covers of the books.

Right from the beginning LOVESWEPT was at the cutting edge, and as our readership changes, we change
with them. In the process, we have nurtured writing
stars, not only for romance, but for the publishing
industry as a whole. We're proud of LOVESWEPT
and the authors whose words we have brought to
countless readers over the last ten years.

The lineup next month is indeed something to
be proud about, with romances from five authors
who have been steady—and stellar—contributors to
LOVESWEPT since the very beginning and one up-
and-coming name. Further, each of these six books
carries a special anniversary message from the author
to you. So don't let the good times pass you by. Pick
up all six books, then sit back and enjoy!

The first of these treasures is **WILDFIRE**, LOVE-
SWEPT #618 by Billie Green. Nobody can set aflame

a woman's passion like Tanner West. He's spent his life breaking the rules—and more than a few hearts—and makes being bad seem awfully good. Though small-town Texas lawyer Rae Anderson wants a man who'd care for her and give her children, she finds herself rising to Tanner's challenge to walk on the wild side. This breathtaking romance is just what you've come to expect from super-talented Billie!

Kay Hooper continues her *Men of Mysteries Past* series with **THE TROUBLE WITH JARED**, LOVESWEPT #619. Years before, Jared Chavalier had been obsessed by Danica Gray, but her career as a gemologist had driven them apart. Now she arrives in San Francisco to work on the Mysteries Past exhibit of jewelry and discovers Jared there. And with a dangerous thief afoot, Jared must risk all to protect the only woman he's ever loved. Kay pulls out all the stops with this utterly stunning love story.

WHAT EMILY WANTS, LOVESWEPT #620 by Fayrene Preston, shocks even Emily Stanton herself, but she accepts Jay Barrett's bargain—ten days of her company for the money she so desperately needs. The arrangement is supposed to be platonic, but Emily soon finds she'll do just about anything . . . except let herself fall in love with the man whose probing questions drive her into hiding the truth. Fayrene delivers an intensely emotional and riveting read with this different kind of romance.

'TIL WE MEET AGAIN, LOVESWEPT #621 by Helen Mittermeyer, brings Cole Whitford and Fidelia Peters together at a high school reunion years after she'd disappeared from his life. She's never told him the heartbreaking reason she'd left town, and once the silken web of memories ensnares them both, they have to decide whether to let the past divide them once more . . . or to admit to a love that time has made only more precious. Shimmering with heartfelt emotion, **'TIL WE MEET AGAIN** is Helen at her finest.

Romantic adventure has never been as spellbinding as **STAR-SPANGLED BRIDE**, LOVESWEPT #622 by Iris Johansen. When news station mogul Gabe Falkner is taken by terrorists, he doesn't expect anyone to come to his rescue, least of all a golden-haired angel. But photojournalist Ronnie Dalton would dare anything to set free the man who'd saved her from death years ago, the one man she's always adored, the only man she dares not love. Iris works her bestselling magic with this highly sensual romance.

Last is **THE DOCTOR TAKES A WIFE**, LOVESWEPT #623 by Kimberli Wagner. The doctor is Connor MacLeod, a giant of a Scot who pours all his emotions into his work, but whose heart doesn't come alive until he meets jockey Alix Benton. For the first time since the night her life was nearly ruined, Alix doesn't fear a man's touch. Then suspicious accidents begin to happen, and Connor must face the greatest danger to become Alix's hero. Kimberli brings her special touch of humor and sizzling desire to this terrific romance.

On sale this month from Bantam are four spectacular women's fiction novels. From *New York Times* bestselling author Amanda Quick comes **DANGEROUS**, a breathtaking tale of an impetuous miss—and a passion that leads to peril. Boldness draws Prudence Merryweather into one dangerous episode after another, while the notorious Earl of Angelstone finds himself torn between a raging hunger to possess her and a driving need to keep her safe.

Patricia Potter's new novel, **RENEGADE**, proves that she is a master storyteller of historical romance. Set during the tumultuous days right after the Civil War, **RENEGADE** is the passionate tale of Rhys Redding, the Welsh adventurer who first appeared in **LIGHT-NING** and Susannah Fallon, who must trust Rhys with her life while on a journey through the lawless South.

Pamela Simpson follows the success of **FORTUNE'S CHILD** with the contemporary novel **MIRROR, MIRROR**. When an unexpected inheritance entangles Alexandra Wyatt with a powerful family, Allie finds herself falling in love. And as she succumbs to Rafe Sloan's seductive power, she comes to suspect that he knows something of the murder she'd witnessed as a child.

In a dazzling debut, Geralyn Dawson delivers **THE TEXAN'S BRIDE**, the second book in Bantam's series of ONCE UPON A TIME romances. Katie Starr knows the rugged Texan is trouble the moment he steps into her father's inn, yet even as Branch is teasing his way into the lonely young widow's heart, Katie fears her secret would surely drive him away from her.

Also on sale this month in the Doubleday hardcover edition is **MOONLIGHT, MADNESS, AND MAGIC**, an anthology of original novellas by Suzanne Forster, Charlotte Hughes, and Olivia Rupprecht, in which a journal and a golden locket hold the secret to breaking an ancient family curse.

Happy reading!

With warmest wishes,

Nita Taublib

Nita Taublib
Associate Publisher

You were entranced by *RAINBOW*,
captivated by *LAWLESS*,
and bedazzled by *LIGHTNING*.
Now get ready for...

Renegade
by
Patricia Potter

"One of the romance genre's greatest talents."
—*Romantic Times*

*A new novel of romance and adventure...a passionate
tale of a scoundrel who becomes a seeker of justice and the
woman who tames his reckless heart.*

When Rhys Redding is freed from a Confederate jail
at the end of the Civil War by Susannah Fallon, he
has no idea that she will demand that he take her
across the lawless South to her home in Texas. As
they traveled the scarred, burned-out land, they
would feel the heat of passion's flame — but once
they reached their destination, would Rhys take
flight again...or would the man who insisted he had
no soul realize that he'd found the keeper of his
heart?

ON SALE IN APRIL
56199-5 $5.50/6.50 in Canada

OFFICIAL RULES TO WINNERS CLASSIC SWEEPSTAKES

No Purchase necessary. To enter the sweepstakes follow instructions found elsewhere in this offer. You can also enter the sweepstakes by hand printing your name, address, city, state and zip code on a 3" x 5" piece of paper and mailing it to: Winners Classic Sweepstakes, P.O. Box 785, Gibbstown, NJ 08027. Mail each entry separately. Sweepstakes begins 12/1/91. Entries must be received by 6/1/93. Some presentations of this sweepstakes may feature a deadline for the Early Bird prize. If the offer you receive does, then to be eligible for the Early Bird prize your entry must be received according to the Early Bird date specified. Not responsible for lost, late, damaged, misdirected, illegible or postage due mail. Mechanically reproduced entries are not eligible. All entries become property of the sponsor and will not be returned.

Prize Selection/Validations: Winners will be selected in random drawings on or about 7/30/93, by VENTURA ASSOCIATES, INC., an independent judging organization whose decisions are final. Odds of winning are determined by total number of entries received. Circulation of this sweepstakes is estimated not to exceed 200 million. Entrants need not be present to win. All prizes are guaranteed to be awarded and delivered to winners. Winners will be notified by mail and may be required to complete an affidavit of eligibility and release of liability which must be returned within 14 days of date of notification or alternate winners will be selected. Any guest of a trip winner will also be required to execute a release of liability. Any prize notification letter or any prize returned to a participating sponsor, Bantam Doubleday Dell Publishing Group, Inc., its participating divisions or subsidiaries, or VENTURA ASSOCIATES, INC. as undeliverable will be awarded to an alternate winner. Prizes are not transferable. No multiple prize winners except as may be necessary due to unavailability, in which case a prize of equal or greater value will be awarded. Prizes will be awarded approximately 90 days after the drawing. All taxes, automobile license and registration fees, if applicable, are the sole responsibility of the winners. Entry constitutes permission (except where prohibited) to use winners' names and likenesses for publicity purposes without further or other compensation.

Participation: This sweepstakes is open to residents of the United States and Canada, except for the province of Quebec. This sweepstakes is sponsored by Bantam Doubleday Dell Publishing Group, Inc. (BDD), 666 Fifth Avenue, New York, NY 10103. Versions of this sweepstakes with different graphics will be offered in conjunction with various solicitations or promotions by different subsidiaries and divisions of BDD. Employees and their families of BDD, its division, subsidiaries, advertising agencies, and VENTURA ASSOCIATES, INC., are not eligible.

Canadian residents, in order to win, must first correctly answer a time limited arithmetical skill testing question. Void in Quebec and wherever prohibited or restricted by law. Subject to all federal, state, local and provincial laws and regulations.

Prizes: The following values for prizes are determined by the manufacturers' suggested retail prices or by what these items are currently known to be selling for at the time this offer was published. Approximate retail values include handling and delivery of prizes. Estimated maximum retail value of prizes: 1 Grand Prize ($27,500 if merchandise or $25,000 Cash); 1 First Prize ($3,000); 5 Second Prizes ($400 each); 35 Third Prizes ($100 each); 1,000 Fourth Prizes ($9.00 each); 1 Early Bird Prize ($5,000); Total approximate maximum retail value is $50,000. Winners will have the option of selecting any prize offered at level won. Automobile winner must have a valid driver's license at the time the car is awarded. Trips are subject to space and departure availability. Certain black-out dates may apply. Travel must be completed within one year from the time the prize is awarded. Minors must be accompanied by an adult. Prizes won by minors will be awarded in the name of parent or legal guardian.

For a list of Major Prize Winners (available after 7/30/93): send a self-addressed, stamped envelope entirely separate from your entry to: Winners Classic Sweepstakes Winners, P.O. Box 825, Gibbstown, NJ 08027. Requests must be received by 6/1/93. DO NOT SEND ANY OTHER CORRESPONDENCE TO THIS P.O. BOX.

SWP 9/92